Magic Kitten

Books 1–2

SUE BENTLEY

illustrated by Angela Swan

Grosset & Dunlap

GROSSET & DUNLAP
An Imprint of Penguin Random House LLC, New York

Text copyright © 2006 by Sue Bentley. Illustrations copyright © 2006 by Angela Swan. Cover illustrations copyright © 2006 by Andrew Farley. *A Summer Spell* and *Classroom Chaos* first published in Great Britain in 2006 by Penguin Books Ltd., and in the United States in 2008 by Grosset & Dunlap. This bind-up edition published in 2020 by Grosset & Dunlap, an imprint of Penguin Random House LLC, New York. GROSSET & DUNLAP is a registered trademark of Penguin Random House LLC. Printed in the USA.

Visit us online at www.penguinrandomhouse.com.

The Library of Congress has cataloged the individual books under the following Control Numbers: 2008017242, 2008017243.

ISBN 9780593225004   10 9 8 7 6 5 4 3 2 1

Magic Kitten

A Summer Spell

SUE BENTLEY

Bradley—my lovely, laid-back blue boy.

Magic Kitten

A Summer Spell

SUE BENTLEY

illustrated by Angela Swan

★ Prologue ★

A flash of bright white light crossed the sky. A shower of silver sparkles fell upon a young white lion. Before the lion had a chance to blink, it was magically changed into a tiny, fluffy, orange kitten.

Just then, an old gray lion ran up to the little orange kitten and bowed his head. "Prince Flame! You have transformed yourself perfectly! Your uncle Ebony will never recognize you now. But you must hurry. He is on his way to find you. If he catches you, he will kill you. He will stop at nothing until he has your throne for himself."

"Cirrus, my friend. Save yourself!" Prince Flame meowed, his emerald eyes flashing. "I will face him."

"Please, Flame. You must stay disguised as a kitten and hide until you are strong enough to fight your uncle on your own."

Flame shivered. "Where should I hide? My kingdom is no longer safe for me. Uncle Ebony's spies are everywhere . . ."

Cirrus laid a paw on the young prince's little orange head. "Go far away. Grow strong and wise. Return when you are ready to claim the Lion Throne for yourself and rid the land of your evil uncle."

Flame gasped as an enormous adult

lion appeared out of nowhere and lunged toward them. The lion's teeth were bared.

Silver sparks ignited in Flame's fur and the kitten meowed as he felt the magic and power building inside him.

The older lion growled and showed his teeth. And just as he leaped onto a flat rock near Flame and Cirrus, there was a bright blue flash of light. Flame heard the lion roar, then felt himself falling. The magic had worked. He was safe for now.

Chapter
ONE

Lisa Morgan gave a sigh as the train drew to a halt. Long Brackby Station had no waiting room. There was just a wooden platform and some steps that led down to the road. She was surrounded by miles of open countryside.

"Great, I'm being dumped in the middle of nowhere," she grumbled. "Thanks a lot, Mom and Dad!"

Her parents had gone to America on business. But Lisa was going to stay with her Aunt Rose, who she hadn't seen since she was a baby.

Lisa scanned the platform. She saw a woman with braids and flowing clothes hurrying toward her. Her heart sank. Aunt Rose was an old hippie!

I bet she has weird ideas about food, Lisa thought glumly. She imagined being force-fed beans, lettuce, and raw carrots. She pictured herself looking all limp and pale. That would serve her parents right!

The hippie woman smiled. She dashed straight past Lisa and jumped on the train.

"Phew!" Lisa breathed, feeling relieved but a bit disappointed. She had actually liked the idea of making her parents feel guilty for not taking her with them.

Just then a voice called out, "Hi, Lisa! I'm over here!"

A thin woman with wavy brown hair was climbing the platform steps. She wore jeans and a yellow T-shirt. She waved at Lisa.

Lisa waved back.

"Sorry I'm late." Rose gathered Lisa up and gave her a big hug. She then held Lisa at arm's length and studied her. "Gosh, aren't you tall for ten years old?"

"Everyone says that," Lisa murmured.

"Dad says I take after him."

"I think you're right." Rose's smile was warm. It made her eyes twinkle. "It's so nice to have you here for the school vacation. We can really get to know each other."

Lisa felt a little better after Rose's warm welcome. But she wasn't ready to let go of her bad mood. "I didn't want to come here. Mom forced me to stay with you."

Rose looked amused. She picked up Lisa's suitcase. "Well—I'd better make sure you enjoy yourself! Long Brackby may not compare with America, but it has a lot to offer. Come on. Let's go home. The car's this way."

Lisa followed her aunt down the steps. The garage was empty. "Did someone steal your car?" she asked worriedly.

"Oh, no. Matilda's over there." Rose pointed across a wide field. "She conked out on me, I'm afraid. That's why I was late."

Lisa craned her neck. She could just see the rounded top of a red car above a hedge. It looked about a hundred miles away!

Rose grinned at Lisa's expression. "It's only a short walk. I'm sure you wouldn't mind stretching your legs after two hours on the train." She opened a big wooden gate and stepped into the field.

Lisa hung back nervously. There were lots of enormous black-and-white cows in the field. "Won't they chase us?" she asked.

"Not if we don't chase them," Rose

joked. "Just follow me. You'll be fine."
She closed the gate behind them and set
off.

After a couple of feet, Rose stopped
suddenly. "Oh, look, how pretty. That's
ragged robin . . ." She pointed to a
clump of pink wildflowers.

"Oh." Lisa almost bumped into her
aunt. She was keeping a wary eye on the
cows. One of them, which seemed about

the size of a bus, was staring hard at her. She was sure it was going to charge at any moment. Rose set off again. "Lisa, you'd better watch out for the . . . ," she began.

Lisa's foot sank right into something soft and smelly. She skidded and almost slipped over. "Ugh! How gross is that!"

". . . cow pies," Rose finished.

"My sneakers!" Lisa wailed. "They're ruined."

Rose's mouth twitched. "Oh, well, it's only a bit of old poo. We can hose it off when we get home. Good thing you didn't slip and fall in it!"

Lisa scowled at Rose. "Ha, ha," she muttered angrily.

Peering down at her sneaker, Lisa hopped on one foot, trying to wipe the sole clean on the grass. When she looked up again, she saw that Rose was almost at the other end of the field.

"Wait for me!" she shouted in panic. She raced across the field and shot through the gate. There was no way she was going to be left behind with the cows, to be trampled into a human pancake!

Rose walked along until she came to her car. "Here we are. Say hello to Matilda."

Rose's VW Beetle was painted black and tomato red. It looked like a giant, rather battered, ladybug.

"Oh—my—goodness," Lisa mouthed silently. "Will that old thing start?"

"*She*, please," Rose corrected.

"Matilda always starts after a rest." She opened the hood, which Lisa saw was actually the trunk, and put Lisa's suitcase inside. When they were both seated, Rose started the engine. "Hurrah! First time!" she cried.

Despite herself, Lisa smiled.

A couple of minutes later, they drove up to a neat thatched cottage. White roses scrambled all over the honey-colored stone walls.

"Leave your sneakers on the front step. You can clean them later," Rose said. "Would you like a cold drink?" Rose asked.

"Yes, please." Lisa followed her aunt through to the kitchen. A big teapot sat on top of Rose's stove. There was also a deep sink and a wooden dresser, but no dishwasher, toaster, or microwave.

"Now, what can I get you?" asked Rose.

"A Coke, please," Lisa said.

Rose frowned. "I'm afraid I've only got lemonade. It's homemade. Would you like to try it?"

Lisa wrinkled her nose, but she was dying of thirst so she accepted a glass. She took a tiny sip. It wasn't as bad as she'd expected.

"Come on. I'll give you the grand tour." Rose led the way into a room filled with afternoon sunshine.

Lisa saw a sofa with big patchwork cushions and lots of bookcases. "Through there is my workroom." Rose pointed toward an open door.

Lisa peered inside. There were shelves piled with folded material, and glass jars crammed with colorful beads and buttons. "I thought Mom said you were an artist."

Rose chuckled. "I'm a textile artist. I make patchwork quilts and wall hangings."

"Oh," Lisa said. That sounded really boring. "What's upstairs?"

Rose explained that there were two bedrooms. One was hers and Lisa would be using the other.

"It's a little small, isn't it?" Lisa said. She was sure Rose's entire cottage would fit into the living room of her parents' apartment in London.

"I like to think of it as cozy," said Rose with a smile. "It suits me just fine. Why don't we sit down and finish our drinks before I show you your room?"

"Okay," Lisa shrugged. She plonked herself down on Rose's squishy sofa. Something didn't seem quite right with the room. Then, with a shock, she realized why. "You don't have a TV!"

"Oh, I don't bother with watching the box. I always have so much to do," Rose said.

Lisa was speechless. She didn't know *anyone* who didn't have a TV.

Rose took one look at Lisa's glum face. She chuckled. "I've got an old set in the closet. I'll get it for you, if you like."

Lisa shrugged. "I don't mind."

Five minutes later, Rose came in carrying a small black-and-white TV. "Here you go."

Lisa just stared. "It's only got four channels!"

Rose frowned. "How many should it have?"

"I don't know. But ours at home has at least thirty."

"Really?" Rose looked astonished.

"However do they fill that many channels? Well, if you don't want it . . ."

"No, I do. I do!" Lisa decided quickly. She watched as Rose set about plugging in the TV. No microwave and a TV that should be in a museum. This vacation was going to be a nightmare.

Chapter
TWO

As Lisa finished stuffing her clothes into a drawer, her aunt called up the stairs.

"Lisa! Why don't you have a look around outside while I'm cooking dinner? There's something that might interest you in the barn."

Lisa padded downstairs in her socks. Rose was in the kitchen by the back door. She gave Lisa some green rain boots. "You can borrow these."

Lisa rolled her eyes. "Oh, good!" she murmured.

Rose chuckled. "They might not be the height of fashion, but they'll keep your feet clean!"

Rose's garden had a long narrow lawn and a big vegetable plot. The old barn was right at the bottom. Lisa wandered down to it. She hoped the barn wasn't dark and creepy and full of horrible spiders.

Just as she opened the door there was a bright silver flash. Lisa thought she saw a large white shape out of the corner of her eye. She turned her head, but saw only a pile of old newspapers.

She pushed the door wide open and poked her head in. A warm, slightly musty smell greeted her. It was somehow familiar. Lisa went right inside. She could see rows of cages and pens. Now she

recognized that smell. It was just like
inside a pet shop.

"Look at all these animals! This is
great!" There were rabbits, guinea pigs,
and even some hedgehogs. "Aunt Rose
must be into animal rescue."

Sacks of animal food were stored on a
bench. Lisa noticed a glow coming from
one of the food sacks. "That's strange."
She went over to investigate.

"Oh!" She gazed in amazement.

A fluffy orange-colored kitten was curled up on one of the sacks. Silver sparkles glittered in the air around it and its whiskers crackled like electricity.

Lisa stared and stared at the kitten. It looked so real. Was it some kind of new toy? No cat in the world sparkled like that.

Suddenly the kitten's eyes shot open. It took one look at Lisa and hurtled into the air on stiff little legs. "Meow! Monster!" it cried fearfully.

"Argh!" Lisa yelled in shock. Did this kitten really just speak?

Lisa took a step back, fell over her own feet, and landed on her bottom in the straw.

The kitten gazed at her with glowing

emerald eyes. Its fur all stood on end.
Silver sparkles crackled all round it.
"What are you?" it demanded in a
velvety meow.

"I'm a girl," Lisa stammered in
complete shock. "What are you?"

But the kitten didn't seem to hear her.
"A girl?" it repeated to itself. "Strange.
You have two legs. No tail or whiskers."

"Of course I don't! I'm not a cat!"
Lisa said. She rose to her feet slowly,
so that the amazing kitten wouldn't run
away. "My name's Lisa Morgan."

"Lisa," the kitten meowed, looking
up at her. It seemed strangely unafraid of
her, despite how tiny it was. "Where is
this place, Lisa?"

"It's a village called Long Brackby,"
she replied. "My aunt Rose lives here.

I'm staying with her for vacation. What are you doing here? Who are you? *What are you?*"

"I am Prince Flame," replied the kitten, sitting up very straight. "Heir to the Lion Throne."

"Wow! Really?" Lisa was having trouble taking everything in. A royal cat. A magic, talking cat. Here, in her aunt's barn! Lisa thought for a moment. She was confused. "Did you say *Lion* Throne? But you're only a kit—" She was suddenly interrupted as Flame pricked up his ears.

"What is that big noise?"

Lisa heard a car go by on the road outside. "Just a car. It's okay. It won't hurt you." She had a sudden thought. "Are you hungry? Aunt Rose must have loads of cat food. I can get you some if you like."

Lisa saw Flame's eyes light up at the thought of food. "You are kind, Lisa. This is a safe place."

He leaped forward. There was a

bright blue flash and a crackle of silver
sparks.

"Oh!" Lisa was blinded for a second.
When her sight cleared, she saw that in
Flame's place stood a young, regal, white
lion. Then just as suddenly as it had
appeared, Flame returned as the fluffy
orange kitten.

"Flame? Was that you?" she gasped.
"You really are a lion prince!"

Flame blinked up at her with wide,
emerald-green eyes. "I am in danger. I
must hide. Will you keep me safe?" he
asked in a tiny meow.

Lisa's heart melted. Flame was
impressive as a royal lion. Disguised as a
kitten he was adorable. "Oh, of course
I will!" Picking him up, she gently pet
the top of his head. Then she paused for
a moment. "But what are you hiding
from?"

Flame placed his tiny paws on Lisa's
chest and looked up at her. "My uncle
wants my throne. His spies seek me here.
He wants—he wants to kill me."

"Well, they'll have to fight me first!"
Lisa said fiercely. "I'll look after you,

Flame," she promised. "You'll be my secret. My secret magic kitten. Although I don't know what I'm going to tell Aunt Rose. She's going to notice you if you live here."

"Notice who?" asked a voice at her side. "Who are you talking to, Lisa?"

Lisa almost jumped out of her skin. She hadn't heard Aunt Rose come into the barn.

Chapter
THREE

"I found Flame asleep on a sack of food. Please can I keep him?" Lisa asked, stroking Flame's tiny ears.

"Flame? I see you've already given him a name." Rose pet the kitten's soft orange fur. "He's beautiful all right. But we should find out where he lives. He's not one of the rescued animals, you know."

"He doesn't have a home or he wouldn't be sleeping in a barn, would he?" Lisa reasoned. She had promised Flame she would take care of him and

there was *no way* she was letting him
down. "If you let Flame live here, I'll
do everything for him. I'll buy his food
with my allowance. He can sleep in my
bedroom. And . . . and . . . I'll clean out
stinky animal cages and everything!"

Rose laughed. "You're determined to
keep him, aren't you?"

"Completely!" Lisa said excitedly. "So—can he stay?"

"You should give him to me then," Rose said. "I'll check him for fleas and ticks before he comes into the house."

"Stupendous! You can stay here. We're going to be best friends," Lisa whispered, giving Flame a quick hug before handing him to her aunt.

"Hello there, you sweet thing." Rose ran expert fingers through Flame's soft coat. "No flea dirt showing, so far." She then turned him over and searched the paler fur on his fat, round tummy. "Good, none there either."

Flame wriggled and meowed in protest.

Lisa had to bite back a grin. She suspected this was the first time a lion prince had been searched for fleas!

Rose finished her examination. "He's clean and in very good condition. I'm sure he's hungry. You'll find food and a feeding dish on that shelf."

"Thanks, Aunt Rose! You're wonderful!" Lisa hugged her aunt on impulse.

Rose gave her a pleased smile. "Anyone would think you'd never had a pet!"

"I haven't. Mom says it isn't fair to have animals in an apartment." Lisa opened a can, forked food into a dish, and set it on the floor.

Flame purred loudly as he munched on the cat food.

"Well, I agree with your mom about pets," Rose said seriously. "Don't get too attached to Flame. You'll have a tough decision to make when you go back to London."

Lisa knew that Rose was right. But it was too late. She had promised Flame she would look after him, and this magic kitten was the one good thing that had happened since her parents had left her here. She didn't want to give him up!

Flame licked his lips when he'd finished the food. He came and rubbed his body against Lisa's legs. She bent down to pet him and he meowed softly, so only she heard him.

"I am safe with you. Thank you, Lisa."

Rose dug a scoop into a sack of rabbit food.

"I'll help." This wasn't exactly Lisa's idea of fun, but she was determined to show that she meant to keep her promise and make certain that Flame could stay.

For the next half-hour she refilled water bottles, chopped vegetables, and replaced soiled straw.

Flame settled down, tucked his paws

beneath his body, and dozed.

"Thanks, love," Rose said later as she and Lisa washed their hands. "I bet you're ready to eat. I know I am."

Lisa scooped up the sleepy kitten and followed Rose back to the cottage. Rose gave her an old blanket and Lisa spread it on the sofa. Flame jumped straight up and began pedaling it into a soft nest with his front paws.

A few minutes later, Rose brought heaping plates of food to the table.

"Er . . . thanks." Lisa poked the food with her knife. It was shepherd's pie with a lot of fresh green stuff next to it.

"That's called salad. We eat a lot of it in the country. It's the law!" Rose kept a straight face.

"I get the message," Lisa said with

a grin. The pie was delicious and she
even ate some of the salad. Afterward,
Lisa went to sit near Flame on the sofa.
"Thanks, Aunt Rose. I think I'll curl up
with Flame and watch TV now."

"Do you mind doing that later?" Rose

said. "House rules are—I cook, you wash up. Okay?"

"Oh, right." Lisa felt herself blush. She jumped up and collected the dishes. Wasn't there even a dishwasher here?

In the kitchen, Lisa filled the sink with hot water and squirted dish-washing liquid over the pots and pans. As she began scrubbing them clean, suds foamed up past her elbows. "Uh-oh," she said worriedly as more suds waterfalled onto the kitchen floor and slopped around her feet. "I think I overdid it! What a mess. Aunt Rose is going to kill me!"

"May I help?" came a tiny voice from the kitchen floor.

She turned to see that Flame stood behind her. His orange fur was fizzing with huge silver sparkles, his whiskers crackled, and his eyes glowed like emerald coals. Lisa felt a hot prickling sensation down her spine.

Something was about to happen!

Chapter
FOUR

Flame leaped up into the air like a silver fireball and landed on the draining board. Sparks crackled from the tips of his ears.

He waved his front paws, and plates, spoons, forks, knives, and pans all dunked themselves in the suds. One by one, they jumped into the air, and spun themselves dry.

Lisa's eyes widened. "Wow! This is *so* cool!"

Cabinet doors flew open and clean plates stacked themselves on the shelves. Drawers opened, so that forks, knives, and spoons could zoom inside.

Lisa watched the suds drain away. The dishcloth did a little dance as it wiped the sink clean. Another cloth shimmied across the kitchen floor. "Look at them go!" She clapped her hands with delight.

"Lisa? Are you all right? There's a lot

of noise in there," Rose called from the living room.

"Oh, no!" Lisa's hand flew to her mouth. She waved frantically at Flame. "Quick. Stop doing whatever you're doing!" she hissed. "I'm fine. Almost finished!" she called to her aunt, in what she hoped was a normal voice.

Crash! Cabinet doors closed. *Bang!* Drawers slammed shut. *Rattle!* Silverware settled into place.

Seconds later, Rose popped her head around the kitchen door. "What *is* going on in here?"

Flame sat on the floor, looking just like a normal orange kitten. Phew! Lisa let out her breath and gave her aunt a rather shaky smile. That was a close call!

"I'm really impressed. The whole

kitchen's spotless. Well done," Rose said admiringly.

"Oh, it was nothing," Lisa said, shining the back of her nails on her T-shirt.

She winked at Flame, who gave a mischievous "meow."

A big bubble of laughter lodged in Lisa's chest. With Flame around, she reckoned this vacation might not be so bad after all.

The following morning, Lisa woke up early. She lay with her eyes closed, listening for the sound of traffic and taxi horns honking in impatience. But only birdsong drifted in on the fresh breeze from the open window. Lisa opened her eyes as she remembered where she was.

Aunt Rose's cottage in Long Brackby. And yesterday she had found a magic kitten in the barn! Now he was curled up asleep with her.

Flame purred softly in his sleep. As Lisa pet him gently, Flame stretched and yawned, showing his little pink tongue and sharp white teeth. Silver sparks glittered in his fur.

"I slept well, thank you," he purred happily.

"Me too," Lisa said as Flame rubbed his head under her chin. "That tickles!" she said with a grin. She pulled herself up out of bed and went in search of the bathroom as Flame made himself comfy on her pillow and waited.

Rose was already in the kitchen when Lisa came down. Lisa fed Flame before she ate her breakfast and then helped Rose clear up, smiling as she remembered how the dishes got cleaned yesterday!

"Do you want to bike to the village store?" Rose asked. "We need milk, bread, and eggs, but I've got tons of sewing to do," she explained. "You could use my bike. It would help me

out and would give you a chance to explore."

"Sounds great," Lisa said. Having Flame along would make even boring old shopping fun!

Rose fetched her bike. It had a deep basket on the front. Lisa lined it with Flame's blanket and then lifted him in.

50

"There. It's just right for you!"

Flame purred softly in agreement.

Rose laughed. "You know, I think that kitten understands every word you say!"

She came around to the front of the cottage to give Lisa directions to the village shops. "Go up Berry Road to the crossroads and turn right. You'll see the White Hart Inn. The shops are just a bit farther on. You can't miss them."

Rose's red and black VW Beetle was parked by the gate. "Hi, Matilda!" Lisa called as she cycled past. "See you later, Aunt Rose!"

The honey scent of hawthorn filled the lane. Skylarks circled overhead, drifting on the warm air. Flame had his nose in the air, sniffing the delicious country smells.

"Now—we turn here," Lisa reminded herself.

Berry Road was narrow and lined with trees. Lisa began to slow down as she approached a sharp bend.

Suddenly a brown and white pony came hurtling toward her. Lisa caught a glimpse of the rider pulling at the reins. The pony's ears were flat against its head. It snorted loudly, flaring its nostrils.

"Watch out!" shouted the rider. "I can't stop him!"

Lisa squeezed the brakes hard so that pebbles sprayed the grass shoulder. Flame dug his claws into the basket to brace himself.

But it was too late. They were going to crash!

Chapter
FIVE

Lisa's bike screeched along the road into the pony. The brakes locked and she was launched into the air. Just as she prepared herself for a very painful landing, there was a silver flash and she landed softly onto what felt like a very soft pillow.

"Oh!" she cried in surprise. She pushed herself shakily to her feet and looked down, but there was just the grass beneath her. That was a close call. Flame must have used his magic to save her! But where was he?

Lisa looked around in panic. In the road she saw the pony was snorting with pain and fear. His rider was trying to calm him down. Aunt Rose's bike lay on its side in the road, the pedals still going around. Flame's crumpled blanket was lying beside it.

Lisa's heart lurched. "Oh, no! Flame!"

But Flame was sitting in the gutter, calmly washing his face. He gave a pleased little meow as she bent down to pet him.

"Oh, thank goodness you're okay!" Lisa said.

"Yeah? Well, Fly's not. And it's all your fault!" shouted the boy who'd been riding the pony. "Why don't you look where you're going?"

Stung, Lisa glared at him. The boy looked about twelve. He had dark brown hair and bright blue eyes. "You were on the wrong side of the road!" she protested angrily, picking up her bike.

But the boy ignored her. "Whoa, there. Calm down, Fly!" he soothed. The pony rolled his eyes and kept lifting one back leg. "Oh, great. Now he's lame! Dad's going to kill me. We don't have any money for vet's bills."

Lisa felt sorry for the pony, but she was still furious with its owner. "You should be more careful how you ride him then! Look at my aunt's bike. The front wheel's all bent!"

Flame finished washing himself. He padded over to Fly. Lisa started forward in alarm. Did Flame realize what danger he was in?

"Get that kitten out of the way. Fly's scared of other animals," the boy warned.

Flame stopped right beneath Fly. He looked straight up at the pony, his emerald eyes sparkling. Fly shifted sideways and gave a nervous blow. Then he dipped his head. Flame purred loudly, closing his eyes with pleasure as Fly snuffed warm breath into his fur.

The boy scratched his head. "Will you

look at that? Fly's really taken to that kitten." He ran a hand down his pony's sore leg. "And his leg seems better now. How did that happen?"

Lisa smiled inwardly as she bent down and picked Flame up. "Thanks for saving me. And making Fly's leg better," she whispered.

"I am glad to help." Flame licked her chin with his tiny pink tongue.

Lisa straightened up. "Oh, well, he couldn't have been that hurt in the first place," she said, trying not to laugh at the boy's confusion.

The boy scowled at her. "Whatever," he said. "Come on, Fly. Let's get going."

"Hey! What about the bike? I can't ride it like that," Lisa said with dismay.

"Tough!" The boy grinned.

Lisa was fuming. She opened her
mouth to reply just as a policeman came
around the corner.

The boy groaned. "Oh, great. It's
Mike Sanders. He kicked me off the field
for playing football last week." He threw
a pleading glance at Lisa. "Okay, I *was*
on the wrong side of the road. I couldn't

help it. Some clothes flapping on a line startled Fly and he bolted."

Lisa folded her arms. "So?" she said.

The boy hesitated. "I'll make a deal with you. You keep quiet about me and Fly and I'll fix your bent wheel."

Lisa grinned. "Done! I'm Lisa. Lisa Morgan." She held out her hand. "And this is Flame."

"John Wood," said the boy. He spat in his palm before he shook hands with Lisa, and gave Flame a pat on the head.

The policeman had reached them by now. Mike Sanders had fair curly hair and a pleasant face. He took in the bike with its bent wheel and gave John a stern look. "Hmm. What have you been up to now?"

John looked down at the road and shuffled his feet. "Nothing," he muttered.

Lisa took a step forward. "It's a good thing John came along," she said quickly. "That's my aunt Rose's bike. The wheel bent when I fell over. John's offered to fix it for me."

"Oh really?" Mike Sanders looked surprised. "Good for you, John. That should keep you out of trouble for five minutes." After checking that Lisa wasn't hurt, he went on his way.

"Phew, that was close," said John. He took hold of Fly's reins. "Let's go. I live just over there."

"Don't say 'thanks' for covering for me, or anything?" Lisa said.

John laughed. His blue eyes sparkled. "Okay, I won't!"

Lisa couldn't help laughing back. "Come on, Flame." She lifted him into

the basket and wheeled the bike along
in a wobbly line. John walked ahead,
leading Fly.

"Down here," John said, heading
down a narrow road that branched over
Berry Road.

Lisa paused for a moment as she looked at a large field filled with caravans beyond an open gate.

John turned around. "Well, are you coming or what?"

Flame gave a happy meow. And Lisa pushed him and the wobbly bike through the gate.

Chapter
SIX

The oldest lady Lisa had ever seen came out of an old-fashioned caravan with fancy carving and red and yellow wheels. She waved at John and called for him to come over.

"That's my great-grandma," John told Lisa. "Come and meet her."

Lisa lifted Flame out of the basket and then laid the bike on its side in the grass. Flame scampered straight up the caravan's sloping wooden steps and began rubbing himself against the old lady's long skirts.

"His name is Flame," Lisa told her.

John had tied up Fly before climbing the steps. He gave his gran a kiss on her cheek. "Hi, Gran!"

The old lady's bright eyes crinkled in a smile. "Come on inside and bring your new friends. The kettle's on," she said as she leaned down to pet Flame. "I bet you'd like a bowl of milk, wouldn't you?"

Flame meowed eagerly.

Once inside the tiny living space, Lisa glanced round. Shiny pots and pans hung on hooks above a tiny stove, which made the room very hot. There was a wonderful smell of woodsmoke and lavender polish.

Flame lapped at his milk. He seemed perfectly at home.

John came and sat near his gran.

"Gran, this is Lisa. She's staying with her aunt in the village. Lisa, meet Violet Wood—she's head of our family. Even my dad's afraid of her. But I reckon her bark's a lot worse than her bite!"

Violet gave a gap-toothed grin. "Here! Don't give away all my secrets!" Around her shoulders there was a black fringed shawl with pink roses on it. Big gold hoops glittered in her ears.

"I like your caravan," Lisa said politely as Violet made tea.

"It's my wagon," Violet corrected. "A true traveler doesn't call their home a caravan."

"Sorry," Lisa said.

Violet looked at her with a gaze as bright and shiny as a robin's. "What you got to be sorry about?"

"Er . . . Nothing," Lisa murmured.

"No reason to say you're sorry then!" Violet crowed.

John chuckled. "Stop teasing, Gran. Lisa's all right. She put a good word in for me with Mike Sanders."

Violet poured strong tea into china cups. "Sanders ain't a bad sort. It's that Robert Higgins you have to watch out for. He's been here again, accusing our men of taking deer. I told him I know everything that goes on around here and there's been no poaching. But he wouldn't have it. He as much as called me a liar to my face!" She sniffed indignantly.

"Who's Robert Higgins?" Lisa asked John.

"Higgins runs the estate for his Lordship," John explained. "That bit of forest at the back of your aunt's cottage is part of it."

"You stay out of his way, John, you hear? He's a nasty piece of work," Violet warned him.

"Yes, Gran." John was serious for a moment and then he turned to Lisa. "Gran used to travel all over the country in this wagon. She's not happy about being here on the official travelers' site."

"I miss the open road too much." Violet's beady eyes brightened. "There was this one time when we was *aitched* up for the night by a river . . ."

"That means camped," John explained, smiling at Lisa.

Violet told them about the old days, when a pony drew her wagon through the country lanes. "All the families would meet up with their relatives at horse fairs. There would be dozens of Woods,

Smiths, Lees, and a hundred other names. Oh, it was grand. In late summer, we'd all travel down to Kent for the hop-picking."

Lisa listened in fascination. A look of contentment settled on Violet's face as she pet Flame's soft coat.

Violet saw Lisa watching closely and said, "Flame's a grand kitten, ain't he?" She closed one eye in a broad wink. "He's just magic."

Lisa's eyes widened in shock. *She knows!* she thought. *Violet knows about Flame!*

"Well, Gran. I've got to get my tools to fix Lisa's bike," John said, apparently not noticing anything. "Thanks for the tea and stories."

"You can bring Lisa and Flame to see

me again." Violet came down the wagon steps to wave good-bye. She stood with Lisa as John walked across to a modern, chrome-trimmed trailer.

"Keep this special one safe," Violet said softly to Lisa as she pet the top of Flame's head. "He'll not be with you long."

Lisa gathered Flame in her embrace. She felt a sharp pang at the thought of not having him around. "I don't want him to leave, ever," she said, her voice quivering.

Violet's eyes sparkled kindly. She patted Lisa's arm. "I know. But his destiny is far from here. When the call comes, he must go. Be thankful that he chose you for his special friend."

Lisa hugged Flame's furry little body close. He purred and licked her chin. She had a lump in her throat. "I am. If I look after him really well, maybe he'll decide to stay here."

A wise but sad look crossed Violet's face. "Maybe," she murmured.

"All done," John said, moving the

bike back and forth. "Good as new!"

He lifted Flame into the basket as Lisa got on the bike. "Thanks. Aunt Rose won't notice a thing. Well—bye for now," she said, and cycled toward the site gate.

"I'm going fishing tomorrow," John called after her. "Want to come?"

Lisa had never been fishing, but she thought it might be better than doing nothing at her aunt's cottage. "Okay. Where should we meet?" she shouted.

"Outside the White Hart Inn near the crossroads. Nine A.M.?"

"See you there!" Lisa waved as she turned into the lane.

The sun was low and trees threw long shadows across the road. "That was quite an adventure, wasn't it?" she said to Flame.

Flame meowed in agreement. He curled his front paws over the basket's rim and peered ahead, ears pricked up and fur sparkling.

At the top of the lane, Lisa paused. "Now. Do we go right or left?"

Suddenly a dark-blue van pulled up,

honking loudly. Lisa jumped with fright. The van's broken side-view mirror was only inches away. With a screech of tires, the van sped off.

"Some people have no manners!" Lisa fumed, turning onto Berry Road.

As she rode toward her aunt's cottage, she suddenly felt like she had forgotten something.

Aunt Rose's shopping!

"Oh, no!" she breathed. "Maybe we still have time to go to the shops."

"We are too late." Flame pointed a paw at the red and black VW Beetle, which was coming toward them.

Matilda drew to a halt. Lisa's aunt leaned out of the window, a furious look on her face. "I want a word with you, young lady!" she said.

Lisa's spirits sank. "Uh-oh," she whispered to Flame.

Chapter
SEVEN

Lisa dragged her feet as she followed her aunt into the cottage. There was no way she could avoid a lecture. Flame padded in behind them.

Rose's cheeks were flushed with anger. "You've been gone for hours, Lisa. I've been frantic, driving around looking for you."

"I didn't realize how late it was," Lisa murmured, wondering what all the fuss was about. She was back now, wasn't she?

"You should have come back and

told me where you were going," Rose
snapped. "You know that I'm
responsible for you while you're here.
I thought you were more grown up than
this."

Lisa felt an uncomfortable twinge of
guilt. "I'm sorry, Aunt Rose. I didn't
think." She told her aunt all about almost
crashing into John on Fly, then going
to the travelers' site and having tea with
Violet Wood.

"I'm amazed you weren't hurt when
you fell off the bike. And you really
should have told me first before going
off with someone you've just met! But it
sounds like you had a good time," Rose
said more calmly. She flopped down on
to the sofa and patted the seat next to
her.

Lisa sat near her aunt and Flame curled up between them. "John's really nice when you get to know him, Aunt Rose. He fixed the broken wheel." Oops. She hadn't meant to mention that.

But Rose didn't seem to notice. She sighed and put her arm around Lisa's shoulder. "No harm done. So let's forget it. But promise me you'll always tell me where you're going from now on."

"I promise," Lisa said, making a cross-my-heart shape with one finger.

Rose smiled, her good humor restored. She jumped up and went toward the kitchen. "Right, I don't know about you, but I'm starving. Could you bring the shopping inside, please?"

"Um . . ." Lisa's face fell. "Now

I'm really going to get roasted," she
whispered to Flame.

Flame meowed and twitched his
whiskers. Lisa saw that huge silver sparks
were popping in the air around him. The
familiar warmth prickled down her spine.

"Flame! You can't . . . can you?"

She dashed outside to where she had

left the bike leaning against the cottage
wall. The bike's basket was crammed
with food. There was bread, milk,
eggs, and even a gooey, homemade
chocolate cake.

"Oh, you star!" Lisa swept Flame up
in a huge hug. She kissed his pink nose.
"You've just saved my life!"

Flame widened his eyes. He stopped in mid-purr. "Are you in danger, Lisa?"

"No. It's just something you say." Lisa giggled.

Rose threw up her hands with delight when she saw the cake. "That's my favorite!"

"My treat," Lisa said, biting back a huge grin. She would have loved to say Flame chose it!

That evening after dinner, Lisa washed the dishes without a second thought. She smiled to herself; she must be getting used to life in the countryside! Afterward, she made a cup of coffee for her aunt and took it into the living room. Flame was curled up asleep on his blanket.

"Thanks. I could get used to this," Rose joked. "So, what did you think of Violet Wood?"

"She's great. I loved her cara— wagon," Lisa corrected herself. "It was really small inside, but with a wood stove and bed and everything. Violet told us some stories about her traveling days."

"I expect it was a wonderful life," Rose said. "It's a shame that some things have to change so much. Violet rules the Wood family with a rod of iron—even the men! She really must have taken to you. I've never heard of anyone from the village being invited to have tea with her."

"Violet loved Flame, too," Lisa said. "But not as much as I do." She glanced at the sleeping kitten, a warm glow filling her chest.

Rose smiled. "The Woods seem like a really nice, friendly family."

Lisa was glad her aunt approved of John Wood and his family. "Do you know Mr. Higgins? Violet didn't seem to think much of him."

Rose snorted. "Robert Higgins isn't a nice man. You'd think twice about getting on his wrong side. He's jumped

83

to the conclusion that the travelers have been poaching deer."

"Violet said she told Mr. Higgins that she was sure none of their men had been poaching deer, but he didn't believe her," Lisa told her aunt. If Violet didn't think any of the Wood family had poached deer, then neither did Lisa.

She jumped up. "I'll go and feed the animals." She tickled Flame gently to wake him up. "Are you coming, Flame?"

Flame yawned and stretched. He purred eagerly and jumped down.

Rose stood up, too. "Thanks, love. I've still got this patchwork quilt to finish. I lost a bit of time going off to look for someone who was late coming home," she said with a twinkle in her eye.

In the barn, Lisa filled food dishes and water bottles and replaced soiled bedding. As she fed chopped carrots to the rabbits and guinea pigs, a thought came to her.

"Where did that magic food come from?" she asked Flame.

"I took it from the shop. Like you wanted," Flame said. He frowned. "Did I do something wrong?"

"No. But I'd better go and pay for it. I still have the shopping money in my pocket. We'll ride over there and deliver it and I'll scribble a note to explain things." Lisa grabbed her shoulder bag. "Come on, Flame. Jump in. We'll only be a few minutes. There's no need to tell Aunt Rose."

Lisa and Flame hurried across the green toward the line of shops. She pushed the envelope through the village store's mailbox.

"Job done," she said happily, patting Flame's soft fur. "I really love having you here with me."

"I like it, too," Flame purred contentedly from the opening of her shoulder bag.

The first stars glinted in the violet sky. A smudge of fading peach light just showed above the church spire.

"It's getting dark," Lisa said worriedly. "We'd better get back before Aunt Rose finds out or she'll ground me for the rest of the vacation!"

She started jogging toward the cottage. There was a sign beside a trail she hadn't noticed before. It read "To Lower Berry Road."

"It must be a shortcut. We'll go that way!"

On one side of the trail there were open fields. Thick woods that were part of the estate Robert Higgins looked after stretched away on the other side.

Lisa had been walking for about five minutes when there was a loud bang.

"Oh!" she gasped, nearly jumping out of her skin. "What was that?"

Flame reared up out of the shoulder bag. The fur along his back stood on end. "Danger!" he hissed.

Lisa's breath came faster. She saw beams of light moving through the trees. There were shouts and men moving toward her. More bangs broke the silence.

"They sound like gunshots," Lisa said

shakily. "Come on, Flame. We're getting out of here!"

She clutched the shoulder bag in her arms so that she could run faster without jostling Flame about. She had taken a couple of steps when a dark-blue van drove up. It screeched to a halt, blocking Lisa's way. Lisa spotted the broken side-view mirror.

"It's that van again!" she whispered to Flame.

The driver leaned out of the side window. He shouted to a man coming out of the trees. "Who's that kid? Go and find out!"

Icy fear curdled Lisa's stomach. She couldn't move.

Chapter
EIGHT

A warm tingle spread over Lisa. She felt the sparks crackling in Flame's fur beneath her hand.

"You are safe," Flame assured her softly.

A moment later, a man dashed up to where Lisa was standing. He stared straight at her. "What kid? There's no one here," the man shouted to the van driver.

Lisa gave a shudder of relief. Flame had made her invisible!

"We must go now," urged Flame.

Lisa didn't need telling twice. She ran past the van, where the driver was still frowning in confusion.

Five minutes later she emerged onto Berry Road. She could see her aunt's cottage. Running the last few feet, she slipped into the back garden and crept into the kitchen.

The sound of her aunt's sewing machine came from her workroom. Lisa stuck her head around the door. "I'm going to my room now, Aunt Rose. I want to read for a while."

Rose looked up with a smile. "Okay, love. Thanks for seeing to the animals. I'll look in on you before I go to bed."

Lisa heaved a sigh of relief as she climbed the stairs. She had only just about stopped trembling. What had those

men in the woods been doing? Maybe
they were shooting crows or rabbits.
They had seemed really angry at being
disturbed.

Thank goodness for Flame. Once
again he had saved her!

★

"Have you made any plans for today?" Rose asked the following morning. Sunshine set rainbow patterns dancing from the crystal hanging in the window.

Lisa told her she was meeting John. "We're going fishing."

"Are you taking Flame with you?" asked Rose.

"You bet!" Lisa said. She wouldn't dream of leaving him behind. Especially after the way Flame had saved her last night.

Flame wound himself around her legs affectionately.

Rose reached down to pet him. "Well, have fun, you two. Be back in plenty of time for supper, okay?"

"Definitely," Lisa promised. "Come on, Flame, jump in." Looping her bag onto her shoulder, she set out for the White Hart.

John and Fly were already waiting when Lisa and Flame arrived. "The river's this way," John said. They went past the green to a line of silvery willow trees.

The river gleamed through the swaying branches. John led the way down a grassy bank. "Our family's got special permission to fish here. Dad helps clear waterweed away in spring."

Flame stretched out in the grass and closed his eyes, purring contentedly. Fly, who was cropping the sweet grass, swung his head around and gave Flame a friendly snort.

"I can't get over how much Fly likes

that kitten," said John, setting out his
fishing things.

Lisa smiled. "Flame's not just any old
kitten. He's really special."

John passed Lisa a fishing rod and a
small, battered can. "You can use my
spare rod. Do you think you can bait it
yourself?"

"Sure! How hard can it be?" Lisa
opened the can. It was full of little,
squirming white bodies. "Ugh! Maggots!"
she gasped.

John grinned. "You nearly dropped
the whole thing! What did you think was
in there, bread crumbs?"

"Something like that!" Lisa admitted,
blushing. "I don't think I can hook one
of these on."

"Give them to me. It's easy. I'll do it

for you." John gave her the baited rod
and showed Lisa how to cast the line
into the river. Lisa soon had the hang
of it and they settled down to wait for a
bite.

The scent of warm grass drifted on

the river breeze. A duck picked her way through the reeds.

"You've got a bite!" John suddenly declared. He reeled in the fish and slipped it into a net in the water. "There you go. One fat brown trout."

"This is fun!" Lisa said. She felt proud of catching her very first fish.

John beamed at her. "You're not bad company for a girl *and* a townie!"

"Watch it! You . . . you road rogue!" Lisa laughed.

"Road . . . what?" John asked as he fell over laughing.

"Hello there! Caught anything yet?" called a voice. Mike Sanders came along the river path, a smile on his pleasant face.

"Not again," John groaned, but he nodded politely.

Mike Sanders peered into the net. "That's a fine dinner for someone."

"Yeah, it's Lisa's first-ever fish," John said.

Mike Sanders smiled at Lisa. "Beginner's luck, eh?" His face suddenly turned more serious. "Now, I don't suppose you've

heard anything about a couple of deer
that were killed last night, John?" he
asked.

John shook his head. "Why ask me?"

"Because I reckon you've got a level
head on your shoulders. You'd know
where to come if you got wind of
anyone poaching around here, wouldn't
you?" Sanders said.

John shrugged. "I might. But I don't
know anything."

"Where were they killed?" Lisa asked.

"In the woods near Lower Berry
Road," Sanders told her. "Near where
your aunt Rose lives." He gave John a
friendly pat on the back. "Well—keep
your eyes peeled." He looked back
before continuing down the river path
and called over his shoulder, "Hope the

fish keep biting."

Lisa stared after him, her thoughts whirling as she remembered the shots in the woods last night and the men with flashlights among the trees. Then there was the blue van, which she had seen twice now.

She had been tempted to tell Mike Sanders her suspicions, but she didn't have any proof. And she'd have to explain what she'd been doing out near the woods at night. That meant risking getting into trouble again with Aunt Rose.

Were those men the deer poachers? She pressed her lips together in determination. She and Flame were going to find out.

Chapter
NINE

Lisa stared out of the cottage window
as drops streamed down the glass. It had
been raining all afternoon. Aunt Rose
was at the village hall running a workshop
on making patchwork quilts. Lisa felt
restless.

Flame jumped onto the windowsill.
He batted at the glass, trying to catch
the raindrops. Lisa laughed and dangled
a piece of wool for him to catch. "You
want to go out, too, don't you? I hope it
stops raining before tonight."

Flame nodded and wrinkled his little

pink nose. "I do not like wet fur."

Lisa planned to wait until dark and then go back up to the woods and have a good look around.

Just then she heard a knock at the kitchen door. It was John on Fly.

Lisa took one look at him. "What's wrong?" she gasped.

John was soaked to the skin. His hair was plastered flat and his face looked pale and angry. "It's my dad. He's been taken to the police station. They think he's been poaching deer," John told her as he tethered Fly to the back porch. He looked like he might burst into tears.

"Oh, that's awful. I'm really sorry," Lisa sympathized. She grabbed a towel so John could dry himself.

John's shoulders slumped as he

sank into a kitchen chair. "It's Robert Higgins's doing. I know it is. But I don't get it. What's he got against my dad? He's never done anything to him."

Lisa bit her lip, wishing she could think of some way to help. She got him a piece of the delicious chocolate cake. "Here you are."

He cheered up a bit as he ate. "Gran's furious, but she's worried, too. If only there was something I could do."

"Maybe there is," Lisa said on impulse.

She told John about the gunfire and the men she'd seen in the woods. "And I've seen that blue van twice. I know it was the same one because of the broken side-view mirror."

John jumped to his feet and paced

around the kitchen. "It must have been the poachers! Deer are big animals. You'd need a van to take them away. Maybe we should go and tell Mike Sanders."

"I thought of that already. But we don't have any proof. Shouldn't we

wait until we're sure about this?" Lisa
reasoned.

John gnawed at his lip. "You're right.
And if the police start going around
asking tons of questions, the poachers
will go into hiding. That leaves my dad
as the chief suspect. But how do we get
proof?"

"I've got an idea . . ." Lisa began
telling him about her plan to go to the
woods after dark.

John listened in silence, then a wide
grin spread across his face. "What time
do we meet?"

"We?" Lisa grinned back. "I hoped
you might say that!"

"You don't think I'd let you have all
the fun, do you?" John said. He got up
and went toward the garden to untie Fly.

Lisa was relieved. It had been really scary up in those dark woods.

"All right," she said. "I'll meet you at midnight on the back path to the woods. Don't do anything before I get there, okay?"

"Who, me?" John flashed her one of his grins. He jumped up onto Fly's back and urged the pony forward. "See you tonight," he called over his shoulder.

The bedroom was dark except for the digital display of her bedside clock. Lisa jolted awake. Flame was licking her chin. His whiskers tickled her nose.

"Thanks for waking me!" She yawned and rubbed her eyes.

"You are welcome," Flame purred, his fur twinkling in the darkness.

It was a quarter to midnight. No time to waste. Lisa was fully clothed beneath the covers. Reaching for her bag and a disposable camera, she and Flame crept downstairs and out of the house.

The moon sailed overhead, as bright as a beacon. Lisa's eyes soon adjusted as she made her way to the woods. Flame trotted beside her. With his cat night-sight he moved as easily as in daylight.

"This is the path," Lisa whispered, pointing ahead. "But look! The blue van's parked near those bushes."

Lisa's heart pounded as she and Flame crept forward. She scanned the path and clusters of trees, looking for John. But there was no sign of him.

Flame pricked up his ears. "There are men in these woods."

A moment later, Lisa heard voices shouting. "Get him! He knows who we are!"

Shadowy shapes crashed through the trees. Someone shoved branches aside and rushed toward Lisa, gasping for breath. For an instant a slim, scared figure was caught in a beam of the flashlight.

Lisa's eyes opened wide with shock. "It's John!"

Chapter
TEN

Almost immediately Lisa felt the familiar tingly warmth down her spine. Silver sparks crackled in Flame's fur and his whiskers glittered in the dark.

"No one can see you, Lisa," Flame explained softly. He hung back, melting into the deep shadows. "Save John."

Lisa let out a sigh of relief. Flame had made her invisible again!

John stumbled out of a thicket right beside her. Leaning against a big oak, he doubled over, clutching a stitch in his side. Lisa could hear the men coming

closer. They would catch John at any
moment. She had to distract them
somehow.

Lisa started to run, her heart
pounding. Her whole body began to
tingle. A rush of heat swept through her.
She felt her muscles bunch as she made
a huge leap forward—and bounded along

on all fours. Strong, tireless legs carried her on. Her hands and feet had become spread pads, which gripped the leaf litter with sharp claws.

She was a huge cat! A huge *invisible* cat!

Night smells flowed over her. The forest came alive. She could see every leaf and blade of grass and hear every tiny movement. The men seemed to move in slow motion. Their breath sounded like rushing water and their footsteps were as loud as drumbeats.

Lisa rushed up behind the first man and slammed into the back of his legs. He yelled with fright as his knees buckled. In a swift movement, Lisa changed direction and launched herself at another man.

"Oof!" The second man fell sideways.

"Grrr!" Lisa growled with triumph.
She tripped up the third man, who fell
over in a jumble of arms and legs.

The three men picked themselves up.
They looked around nervously. "There's

something weird in here!" one said.

Lisa grinned. She crept up close behind them and opened her mouth wide. "Grrr-owl!!" she roared.

"What's that?"

"I don't know, but I'm out of here!" one of them cried. "Get back to the van!"

Lisa knew that John was safe for the moment. Time to get the evidence they needed.

She bounded swiftly toward the parked van and reached it ahead of the men. The back door was ajar. Her cat senses caught the smell of death. Two deer lay in the back of the van. Lisa jumped inside, already fumbling for her camera. Her fingers closed around it.

Fingers? She wasn't a cat anymore!

Flame's spell must have worn off. Did that mean that the men could see her now?

There was no time to think. Aiming the camera, she took a photo of the dead deer. Suddenly, the back door was wrenched open behind her. But Lisa was ready. She stuck the camera in the men's faces. *Flash! Flash!* She took their photos.

"Wassat?" one yelled, covering his face with his hand.

"I can't see. I'm blinded," moaned another, hopping around and bumping into his friends.

Lisa leaped out and dashed behind a tree. Moments later, the engine fired up and the van sped off up the road.

Lisa leaned against the tree and gave a nervous shaky laugh. Wow! That was

close. She loved being a cat! She couldn't
wait to talk to Flame all about it.

She glanced around for him. Where
was he? He usually kept close beside her.
As she made her way back toward the
road, she called softly, "Flame. Where are
you?"

"I am here," came a tiny whimper.
Flame crawled out from beneath some
ferns. His eyes were wide with alarm.

Lisa picked him up. "Oh, you're
trembling." She pet his head and gave
him a cuddle. "Don't be scared for me.
Your magic was amazing! Those horrible
men have left."

But Flame nestled closer, his tiny heart
beating fast. Lisa felt a stir of unease as he
gave another little whimper.

Just then John ran up to her. "Lisa?

Where have you been? You missed all the fun!" he panted. "I know who the poachers are!"

Lisa gently tucked Flame into her shoulder bag. He would be warm and safe in there. "Did you get a good look at them?" she asked.

John's face was white, except for a smudge of dirt on his cheek. He nodded. "Two of them are friends of Higgins's! He must be in on it. No wonder he's trying to blame my dad. They tried to catch me, but I lost them in the woods."

"I'm just glad you're safe," Lisa said, relieved that they were both okay.

John frowned. "I might be safe, but I still don't have any proof. It's my word against theirs."

Lisa felt in her pocket for the camera.

She imagined the look on John's face when he found out she had taken photos. But her fingers closed on nothing but empty space.

Oh, no! The camera wasn't there. She must have dropped it in the woods!

"Photos? How did you get photos? You just got here!" John frowned at Lisa in puzzlement when she had explained.

Lisa thought quickly. She couldn't let John know about Flame's magic. "I saw the blue van on my way to meet you. No one was around. So I risked taking some photos. But I nearly got caught when they came back!"

John looked impressed. He whistled through his teeth. "Those photos will prove my dad had nothing to do with poaching deer. We really need to find that camera. I'll look over where the van was parked."

"Okay. I'll look over here." Lisa went a little way into the woods. Opening her shoulder bag, she whispered to Flame, "Can you help me find the camera, please? I have to be getting back. Aunt Rose will be furious if she finds out I've sneaked out here at this time of night!"

Flame was curled into a tight ball in one corner. He lifted his head and gazed at her with fearful eyes. "I must hide. My enemies are close. Uncle Ebony's spies are almost here," he meowed.

"Oh, no!" Lisa's chest constricted. No wonder Flame was acting strangely. He was in terrible danger.

Chapter
ELEVEN

"You have to leave here, Flame!
Now!" Lisa urged in a shaky voice. Tears
pricked her eyes. The thought of her
friend leaving was heartbreaking. But
Flame's life was in danger and she knew
he must go.

Flame shook his head. His eyes were
dull and his fur was flat. "I am too weak.
I need strong magic to find a new place
to hide soon. But not now," he told her
in a small voice.

Lisa gulped back tears. She was secretly
relieved that they could be together a

little longer, but she was still worried for
his safety. She pet his little velvety ears.
"Please be careful, Flame. I couldn't bear
it if they found you."

Turning his head, Flame touched the
tip of Lisa's index finger with his nose.
"You must find the camera."

Lisa's finger felt warm and tingly
and the end began glowing softly. She
understood what she must do.

Flame's head drooped and he curled
back into a tight ball. Lisa saw with
dismay that only two or three little silver
sparkles glinted in his fur.

There was no time to waste. Lisa
clutched her shoulder bag to her side and
began searching for the camera, using her
glowing finger as a guide. She pushed
leaf mold aside and poked under fallen

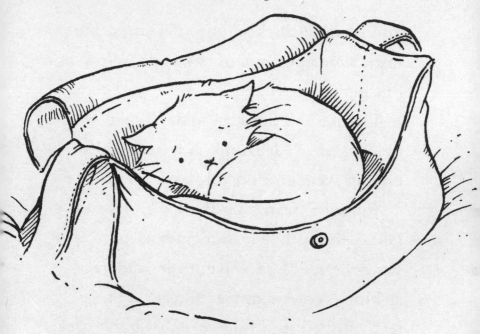

twigs. As she moved toward a tuft of
grass, her finger stopped glowing. "I must
be getting cold."

She turned back toward a group of
birch trees and her finger glowed faintly.
"Now I'm getting hotter."

She kept searching, watching for her
magic finger to give her clues. As she

stood over a thick clump of ferns, a big spark shot right out of the end. "Wow! I'm boiling now!"

Lisa pushed the fern aside. There was the camera. "Amazing!" She scooped it up and went to find John.

John was searching the long grass beside the path. He straightened up when he saw Lisa waving the camera at him. "You've got it? Great!" His teeth flashed in a huge grin. "I'll get the photos developed first thing tomorrow morning. Gran will come with me to see Mike Sanders. I would like to see anyone argue with her, once they see the photos! Thanks a million, Lisa."

Lisa blushed. "Glad we could help."

"We?" John said, looking a little confused.

"Me and Flame," Lisa said.

"Oh, yeah!" John chuckled. "Thanks, Flame. You'd better go now. Your aunt will skin me alive if she finds you out here with me!"

Lisa smiled and waved good-bye as she hurried back to her aunt's cottage.

She didn't see the long black shadows prowling through the trees. Two large black cats appeared for an instant. One of them lifted its head, scenting the air before they both disappeared.

There came a faint echo of a powerful voice. "The prince is near. We are close . . ."

Lisa crept in the back door and up through the darkened cottage.

"Phew, made it," she breathed, closing

her bedroom door behind her.

Now that the excitement was over, she felt really tired. She undressed and crawled into bed. Flame jumped up and settled down beside her. He reached forward and touched her chin gently with the tip of his cold, pink nose.

"You are a good friend, Lisa," he said with a rumbling purr. "I will never forget you."

A hard ball of misery lodged in her chest and her eyes filled with tears, but she swallowed them bravely. "Me too. I've loved having you here, Flame. But I know you have to leave soon."

"Soon," Flame agreed sadly and snuggled up under her chin.

Moments later, Lisa fell deeply asleep.

★

The next day, Lisa was in the barn.
She was filling dishes with scoops of
pet food and trying not to think about
Flame leaving. She knew she should be
feeling happier—she had heard from her
aunt earlier that day that Higgins and his
friends had been arrested. But she was
just so sad at the thought of losing Flame.
Right then he was sitting on the sack of
food where she had first discovered him,
his eyes watchful and intent. He kept
lifting his head, testing the air for his
enemies' scent.

Lisa had her arms full of hay when she
heard her aunt calling. "Lisa! You've got
visitors!"

She looked up to see her aunt and
two other people coming into the barn.

"Mom! Dad!" she cried with delight

as she ran toward them and threw herself into their arms. "What are you doing here?"

Mrs. Morgan laughed. "We missed you. So we came back early. Rose has asked us to stop by for a few days before we all go back to London." She turned to her sister with a smile.

"You don't mind, do you, love?" asked Mr. Morgan, looking a bit worried. "I know you've probably been really bored here in the country."

Lisa realized that she had enjoyed herself far more than she ever thought possible. And this was mainly due to Flame. She was about to reply that she'd had a fantastic time when she noticed a flash of light from near the sack of food.

"Why don't you go into the kitchen?"

she said hurriedly. "I'll finish feeding the animals, then I'll come, too."

Rose led Lisa's parents out of the barn. "Let's leave Lisa to it. She always insists on getting her chores finished by herself. She's been a great help to me."

"Really? That doesn't sound like the grumpy girl we dropped off at the train station last week!" Lisa's dad said with surprise.

"She certainly looks a lot happier than I expected!" said her mom, looking slightly amazed. "See you in a minute," she called over her shoulder.

As soon as they had left, Lisa spun around. She ran toward the back of the barn and stopped in her tracks, stunned by what she saw.

An enormous young white lion with

glowing emerald eyes stood there. His fur glittered and sparkled and his whiskers glowed with light. Prince Flame was no longer disguised as a fluffy orange kitten. Beside him stood an older-looking gray lion, a calm expression on his wise face.

As Lisa watched, silver sparks filled the air. The two lions began to fade. Prince Flame lifted his paw in a final wave. His mouth curved in a gentle smile.

"Be well. Be strong, Lisa," he said in a deep growling purr.

Then he was gone.

Lisa stood there, a wave of deep sadness flowing over her. She wondered where Flame would go now to hide. Would he ever be safe from his uncle's spies? Would he one day rule his strange, magical land?

"Good-bye, Prince Flame," Lisa whispered. "Take care. Stay safe. I'll never forget you."

She stood there for a moment longer, thinking of the wonderful adventure she and Flame had shared. Even though her heart was aching, she knew she wouldn't have changed a single moment.

At last, she took a deep trembling breath. Her parents were waiting for her. She knew she would never tell them or anyone else about Flame. He would always be her very own magical secret. But there was still so much more to tell them. And she couldn't wait for them to meet John and Fly.

Magic Kitten

Classroom Chaos

SUE BENTLEY

Brian—the shy blue twin.

Classroom Chaos

SUE BENTLEY

illustrated by Angela Swan

Prologue

As Cirrus and Prince Flame hid in
a cave, the old lion sensed something
strange. "Your uncle is close by, Prince
Flame. You must disguise yourself again! It
isn't safe for you to be here," Cirrus called
to the young lion.

Flame's fur crackled with silver sparks.
There was a dazzling white flash and
suddenly the lion disappeared. In his place
now stood a tiny, fluffy, black-and-white
kitten.

Cirrus leaned down and brushed his old
gray muzzle against the top of the kitten's

fluffy head. "You must go back to the other world, Prince Flame. But stay in this kitten disguise. It will serve you well and keep you hidden from your evil uncle."

Suddenly Flame and Cirrus heard a menacing growl. Flame looked up at Cirrus with his emerald-green eyes. "Uncle Ebony rules my kingdom. One day I will return and claim my throne!" he meowed bravely.

Cirrus's worn teeth flashed in a brief smile. "Yes you will, my prince. But only once your magic powers have become stronger. But for now, you must go and hide!" he cried.

Just as Flame scrambled to hide behind a rock, an enormous adult lion burst through the waterfall in the cave. His huge paws thudded on the ground.

"Cirrus! Tell me where my nephew is hiding! I must find him," Ebony demanded.

Flame's tiny body trembled in fear as he listened from behind the rock.

Cirrus growled. "Prince Flame is far away now. You will never find him!" he responded.

Ebony roared with rage. "My spies are looking for him. Flame cannot hide from me forever . . ."

Behind the rock, Flame felt the magic power building inside him. He let out a tiny meow as silver sparks ignited in his black-and-white fur. The cave began to fade, and he felt himself falling. The magic had worked once more . . .

Chapter
ONE

"Bye! See you at the end of the semester!" Abi West called to her parents from the upstairs window.

As the car pulled out of Brockinghurst School's parking lot, Abi turned back to her new room. She felt excited but a little nervous. It was going to be strange to share a room with someone she didn't know.

"Might as well unpack," she decided, lifting her suitcase onto one of the beds.

There were two single beds with blue

quilts and night tables. Blue-checked
curtains and a red rug made the room
bright and cozy.

From the window, she saw that more
cars were pulling into the front parking

lot. Girls in uniform were getting out and saying good-bye to their families.

Abi had just finished putting away her clothes and books when the door crashed open with a bang.

A pretty, fair-haired girl marched into the room. She scowled at Abi. "Who are you?"

"Hi," Abi said. "I'm Abi West."

"Well, you're in my room," the girl said rudely.

"I thought I could choose any room," Abi said. "I just put all my stuff away."

The other girl put her hands on her hips. "And I'm supposed to care? You'll just have to move it then!"

Abi blinked at her, unsure what to do. The other girl looked about eleven, a year older than Abi.

"I thought I heard your voice, Keera Moore," said a calm voice from the doorway.

Abi spun around. She saw a tall woman with a pleasant face. It was Mrs. York, the head teacher. There was a small, thin girl with her.

Keera changed completely. "Oh, hello, Mrs. York," she said with a smile. "Abi here was just saying she didn't mind moving to another room."

"No, I wasn't!" Abi said indignantly. "You told me this was your room. And that I had to move out!"

Keera glared at her, her blue eyes flashing. "You little tattletale," she hissed.

"That's enough, Keera," the teacher

said. "You know very well that rooms are never reserved at Brockinghurst." She turned to Abi. "Abi West, I want you to meet Sasha Parekh. I thought it might be a good idea for you two to share this room. You'll both have a lot in common. It's the first time either of you has been away from home."

"Ugh," Keera sneered under her breath.

Abi smiled at Sasha, who was very pretty with dark eyes and olive skin. She wore her thick black hair in a long braid. On one cheek she had a red birthmark.

"It's really nice to meet you," Abi said. Sasha seemed a hundred times nicer than Keera already!

"You too," Sasha said shyly.

"I have some animal posters to put on the wall. Would you like to help me?" Abi asked.

Sasha's dark eyes lit up. "Definitely! I love animals."

"So do I. Especially big cats," Abi said, warming to Sasha.

Keera pointed a finger at her open mouth and made pretend gagging sounds.

Mrs. York frowned at her. "This room seems to be taken, Keera. I suggest you try the one next door. It's identical to this one."

"Oh, all right." Keera rolled her eyes as she stomped outside with her suitcase. Mrs. York turned back to Abi and Sasha. "I'll leave you two to settle in. Come down to the hall when you hear the bell. You'll meet your teachers and

get your schedules."

"She's nice, isn't she?" Abi said to Sasha after Mrs. York had left.

Sasha nodded.

Suddenly a lot of banging came from

the room next door. Then a voice
complained, "This is an ugly room! And
this school is a smelly dump! I hate being
back here!"

Sasha looked at Abi. "Keera!" they
said. The two of them began laughing.

"Phew! There's so much to
remember," groaned Abi. She sat down
next to Sasha at a table in the main hall.

The room had wooden beams and
walls of dark, carved wood. An enormous
fireplace took up most of the end wall.
The room was buzzing with girls and
teachers, and everyone seemed to be
talking at the same time.

Sasha bit her nails nervously. "I can't
remember any of the teachers' names or

where the classrooms are."

"I can't either. But I think we'll get used to it soon," Abi said.

"Well! If it isn't the tattletale," a voice behind her said.

Abi didn't need to turn around to know who it was. "Hello, Keera," she said.

Keera came up and leaned her elbows on the table. She was with two other girls. One had brown hair and freckles and the other was tall and thin with black curly hair.

Abi remembered hearing their names called out earlier that day: Marsha Clarke and Tiwa Rhames.

"Did you bring your teddy bears to help you sleep?" Keera said in a mocking, baby voice.

Tiwa snickered. "After all, we wouldn't want you to have nightmares about the ghost."

"What ghost?" asked Abi. "You're making it up. There's no such thing."

Keera smirked. "Oh, no? Haven't you heard about the Gray Lady of Brockinghurst? She haunts the school's hallways, waiting for bratty little first-years. I'd watch out if I were you!" She turned to Marsha and Tiwa. "Come on, let's go and see if the store's open."

The girls nudged each other and laughed as they walked away.

Sasha glanced nervously at Abi. "Do you think there really is a ghost?" she asked. "Most old buildings are supposed to be haunted, aren't they?"

Abi smiled at her as she gathered up all the papers she'd been given. "Keera was just trying to scare us. Don't look so worried." She turned to her backpack. "Oh, I forgot the folder for our next class. I'll just run upstairs and get it."

"Okay. I'll wait here," Sasha said, looking more relaxed now.

Abi found the nearest doorway and went out of the hall. Hurrying past a row of classrooms, she found a narrow stairway. Five minutes later, after countless twists and turns, Abi stopped on a gloomy landing.

"Oh, great! I'm totally lost," she said aloud.

Abi looked around. Narrow windows

of thick glass were set into the walls. Dust swirled in the shafts of light that managed to get through. In front of her there was an old door, covered with cobwebs. She pushed at it with her fingertips. It slowly creaked open.

She looked into the gloom, where dark shapes were visible. As her eyes adjusted to the darkness, she saw stacks of old furniture. It was just an old storeroom.

Then suddenly Abi caught something out of the corner of her eye—something pale and glowing. She gasped. It must be the Gray Lady!

Frozen where she stood, Abi gradually began to realize the glow wasn't actually human-shaped at all. But what could it be?

She crept farther into the storeroom.
Something was lying across two whole
chairs. Abi frowned—it looked like a
sparkly furry blanket. As she took another
step she heard a low rumbling purr.

Abi blinked in disbelief. The "blanket"
looked like a young white lion! He was
fast asleep.

She stared at the silver sparkles
gleaming in the lion's fur. He looked
fierce but beautiful. Abi's heart beat fast.
She didn't know whether to stay or run
away.

"How did a lion get in here?" she
whispered to herself.

The white lion's eyes flew open. He
lifted into a crouch. The hair along his
back stood up in a spiked ridge.

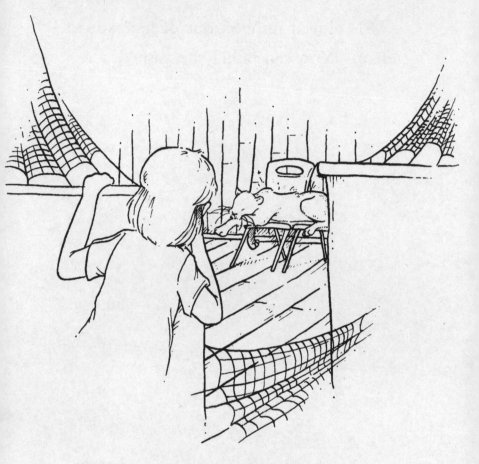

"Don't come any closer! My teeth
are sharp and my claws are strong!" he
growled.

Abi almost jumped out of her skin in terror. "You can talk!" she gasped.

Chapter
TWO

At first the lion just stared at Abi with its piercing emerald eyes.

Abi sensed that it was more frightened than angry. She crouched down to make herself seem smaller. "It's okay. I won't hurt you," she said softly.

The lion relaxed and pricked up its ears. "I do not mean to scare you. I thought you were an enemy," he said in a deep, velvety growl.

"What . . . ? Who are you?" Abi stammered.

"Flame." The lion dipped his head in greeting. "Prince Flame. Heir to the Lion Throne," he told her solemnly.

Abi dipped her head in return. It seemed like the right thing to do. "Where are you from?"

"Far away," Flame replied with a sad look in his eyes.

Abi began to recover from her fear of Flame. She took a step forward and reached her hand out. "I'm Abi. This is my first semester at boarding school. Is it okay if I touch you . . . ?"

"Wait! Stay back!" Flame ordered.

There was a silver flash.

"Oh!" Blinded, Abi put her hands over her eyes. When she looked again, she saw that the white lion had

disappeared. In his place stood a fluffy,
black-and-white kitten with emerald-
green eyes.

"Where's Flame?" Abi gasped.

"I am Flame," the kitten meowed in

a tiny voice. "This is my disguise. I am in hiding. My uncle Ebony is trying to find me. To kill me."

"But why would your uncle want to kill you?" Abi asked.

"He wants to steal my throne. Can you help me, Abi?"

"Of course I will!" She leaned forward and picked up the kitten. "You can live in my room. Just wait until Sasha sees you!"

Flame wriggled. He reached up a tiny paw and touched her chin. "No! You can tell no one. It must be our secret," he urged.

Abi frowned. She felt sure that Sasha could keep a secret.

"You must promise," Flame insisted.

He blinked up at her with wide, trusting
eyes.

Abi felt her heart turn over. She
didn't want to do anything that put him
in danger. "Okay, I promise," she agreed.

Then she had a sudden thought.
Students weren't allowed to have pets.
How was she going to sneak Flame into
her room?

Abi tucked Flame under her sweater.
"Sorry. I have to do this," she said as
the kitten looked up at her indignantly.
"Don't move now, okay?"

Luckily, most of the students were still
in the main hall. She managed to find
her way back to her room without being
seen.

"Here we are," she whispered, putting Flame on her bed.

Flame's eyes scanned the room and then he gave a whiskery grin. "A safe place," he meowed, pointing a black-and-white paw at the bureau.

"You want to go up there?" *It is a good idea*, Abi thought. If he slept at the back against the wall, he'd be out of sight unless someone stood on the bed. "Okay. I'll find something soft to make you a cozy nest."

As Abi began searching in a drawer, Flame's ears pricked. He gave an urgent little meow. "Abi! Someone is coming."

"Oh, no!" Abi whipped around. She saw the door handle turning. There wasn't enough time to hide Flame!

Suddenly Abi felt a strange, tingly
feeling down her spine. Silver sparkles
leaped from Flame's fur and his whiskers
crackled. Little points of light popped in
the air around him.

Something very strange was
happening.

Keera stuck her head around the door.
"I thought I heard voices in here." She
looked straight at the bed where Flame
sat!

Abi's breath caught in her throat.
Keera would tell the head teacher about

Flame! Before she could say anything,
Keera spoke up.

"I thought so!" Keera's mouth twisted
in a triumphant grin. "There's no one
else in here! You're such a big baby,
Abi West. Wait until I tell everyone that
I caught you talking to your imaginary
friend!"

Abi looked back at the bed in
confusion. Flame sat there large as life,
but Keera couldn't see him!

She turned back to Keera. "Tell them
what you like! See if I care," she said.

Keera looked disappointed. She turned
around and slammed the bedroom door
in a huff. Abi heard her walking down
the hallway.

Flame began calmly washing his face.

"How come Keera didn't see you?" Abi asked him.

Flame rubbed a paw across his whiskers. "Magic. I choose who sees me," he explained.

"You mean you can make yourself invisible? That's going to make things much easier. It's always really busy in school and since there're no pets allowed, it's probably best if you only show yourself to me. Okay?" Abi grinned at Flame as he nodded that he understood. "This is fantastic! It's going to be so much fun having you here!"

Flame purred back in agreement.

Chapter
THREE

The next few days passed by quickly. Abi was kept busy with classes, making new friends, and finding her way around. She and Sasha got along really well. She wished Flame could show himself to Sasha, too, but for Flame's safety and the sake of the school rules, the fewer people who knew the better.

Flame came everywhere with her. During classes, he curled up on a nearby windowsill or jumped on top of a bookcase. Abi loved having him around.

He was her special invisible secret. It was
only at night when she lay in bed that
she felt homesick.

Flame snuggled up next to her. Abi
cuddled him and Flame closed his eyes
and purred softly. "Are you homesick,
too?" she whispered, petting his soft fur.

"I miss my good friends." Flame nodded with a sigh.

Abi kissed the top of his head sleepily. It was comforting to hug his warm little body. "We'll just have to look after each other."

Abi awoke one morning to find Sasha already up and dressed. "Yay! It's Saturday! No classes. A day to ourselves," Sasha said, grinning. "What should we do?"

Abi's hands flew to her face. "Yikes! I almost forgot. It's basketball practice! They're choosing teams today." She jumped out of bed and began throwing her clothes on.

Flame sat on the windowsill. The morning sun made his black-and-white coat gleam softly.

"Do you mind if I come?" Sasha asked.

"Of course I don't! But I didn't think you liked basketball," Abi said, stuffing her gym shoes into her sports bag.

Sasha grinned. "I don't! I'm terrible at sports. But I like watching. I can be your number-one fan, if you like!" she joked.

"As if!" Abi laughed and gave her a friendly shove.

Right after breakfast, Abi and Sasha made their way to the school gym. Flame had decided to come, too. He was curled up in Abi's sports bag.

Some other girls from Abi's classes were in the locker room. They called out a greeting to Abi. "Hi!"

"Hi!" Abi answered with a smile. She

changed into her shoes. "Will you be all right?" she whispered to Flame.

"I will be fine. Go and look around," he meowed softly.

Abi ran onto the court where some girls were already practicing their shooting skills. She saw Keera throw the ball straight into the net.

"Good shot," shouted Marsha.

Sasha, who was standing on the sidelines next to Keera's other friend, Tiwa, gave Abi an enthusiastic wave.

Keera looked smug. "In case you didn't know, I'm the school's star shooter," she told Abi.

Miss Green, the gym teacher, blew her whistle. "Gather around, everyone. As you probably know, we play High

Five basketball. So let's divide up into squads. I want to see some teamwork."

Abi put on a jersey with the letters GS, for goal shooter. She really liked High Five. It meant she got a chance to play in all the different positions.

Keera and her friends put on their jerseys. Tiwa said something to Keera, who gave Abi a sly look.

On the whistle, the center passed the ball. Abi and her goal-attack teammate worked to get the ball into the circle. Abi saw an opening. She spun around, aimed, and scored.

"Great job, Abi!" called Sasha.

"Huh! Lucky shot," shouted Tiwa.

Abi scored twice more. She was breathing hard when the timekeeper

called first quarter, but she was eager for
the next game. She loved playing with
her new classmates.

"Switch positions, everyone!" Miss Green called out.

Abi changed to goalkeeper, and on the other team Keera was playing goal attack. She was really good. Abi had to work hard defending against her. Suddenly Keera broke free. She shot at the hoop. The ball bounced off the net.

"Too bad!" called Tiwa.

Keera's face twisted. She looked down at the floor and clenched her fists.

As Abi went after the ball, she saw Flame come bounding up the gym. He jumped on a pile of gym mats. Rolling over, he lay stretched out on his back, showing his pale tummy.

Abi couldn't help chuckling. Flame seemed to be really enjoying himself.

She came and stood behind the line, ready to throw the ball in.

"Were you laughing at me?" Keera demanded.

"No," Abi said, puzzled.

Keera scowled. "You'd better not be. I hardly ever miss a shot at the net."

As Abi threw the ball, she suddenly realized that Keera had seen her laughing at Flame. She was going to have to be a lot more careful at keeping him a secret.

Moments later, Keera caught a low pass from Marsha. Abi was watching her closely. As Keera twisted around, she seemed to slip. Her elbow shot out and jabbed into Abi's ribs.

"Oh!" Winded, Abi doubled over in pain.

"She did that on purpose!" Sasha yelled, forgetting to be shy. Her long braid swung around as she jumped up and down in protest.

"Abi's pretending! That didn't hurt," called Tiwa.

Abi held her side, trying to catch her breath.

She heard a low growl. From the corner of her eye, she saw Flame's fur sparkle and his whiskers crackle with electricity. A warm tingling flowed down her spine.

"Uh-oh," breathed Abi. "Now what?"

Keera aimed the ball at the net, gathered herself to jump, then sprang into the air. She threw the ball. Up it went, higher and higher. "No!" she cried as the ball whizzed right up to the roof beams.

Abi watched in amazement as the ball turned slowly in the air and then zoomed downward. It hit Keera on the head.

"Ow!" cried Keera. Suddenly she started to spin around. She spun faster and faster, until she was just a blur!

Chapter
FOUR

The gym erupted with laughter. Sasha laughed, too, her hands over her mouth.

"Help! I can't stop!" Keera wailed, her arms waving around and her gym shoes squeaking as she pirouetted like a skater on ice.

Miss Green made a sound of impatience. "Keera Moore! Do you always have to be the center of attention?"

Abi had caught her breath by now. She held back a grin. No one else could see Flame. There he sat beneath the goalpost, blinking up at Keera. She edged toward him. "Flame," she gently scolded.

"She hurt you, Abi." Flame's eyes glittered mischievously as the silver sparks made a fizzing noise around him and died down.

"I'm okay now," Abi said. "You can stop spinning her now."

Flame hesitated. He pointed a paw at Keera.

Keera came to a sudden stop and stood there swaying gently. "What happened?" she groaned.

Marsha and Tiwa ran over to help her. "Are you all right?"

"Of course I am! Get off me!" snapped Keera, red-faced with embarrassment.

"What a show-off! I bet she feels sick after all that spinning!" Sasha came over to Abi.

Miss Green clapped her hands. "Drama's over! Take a break, everyone. Gather around. I want to talk to you."

Abi took a cup of water from the fountain and then went and sat near Sasha.

"Every year we pick a team captain," Miss Green was saying. "Brockinghurst is hosting a High Five competition at the end of the semester. So it's especially important that our captain is someone who inspires others to do their best . . ."

Keera looked smug. She shifted around as if ready to get up.

". . . so I've decided that this year it'll be—Abi West!"

Keera's jaw dropped. "But—she's only a first year!"

"Stand up, Abi," said Miss Green, frowning at Keera. "I was impressed by the way you played, and you kept a cool head under pressure. That's the kind of captain we need."

"Me?" Abi gasped in surprise as she

rose to her feet. She felt herself blush.

"Well done, Abi," said Miss Green with a warm smile.

Everyone, except Keera and her friends Marsha and Tiwa, clapped and cheered. Sasha shouted loudest of all.

Abi ate her lunch quickly and then hurried to her room.

Once inside, she poured some milk into a saucer. "There you are. It's a special treat," she told Flame.

Flame purred with pleasure. He lapped the milk with his little pink tongue. When he finished drinking, he curled up on her bed and closed his eyes. "I am sleepy now," he meowed softly.

Abi pet him. "Take a nap. I'm going

to the library. I'll see you later." She picked up a folder and tucked it under her arm.

The library was quiet, so Abi had her choice of the computers. She opened her folder and got to work.

Sasha found her there an hour later. "I've been looking everywhere for you." She peered over Abi's shoulder. Her dark eyes opened wide. "Homework? On a Saturday afternoon?"

Abi felt herself get hot. She hesitated, biting her lip. "Sometimes I need to go over things a few times before I understand them," she admitted after a long pause. "I bet you think I'm stupid, don't you?"

Sasha shook her head. "Of course I

don't! Everybody learns in different ways. Anyway, so what? You're awesome at sports. I could help you if you like."

"Really? That would be great!" Abi beamed at her friend. Sasha was great at schoolwork.

They went through the class notes together. After another twenty minutes,

Abi sat back. "It makes so much more sense now."

"See, you can do it," Sasha said with a smile. "Do you want to walk into town? We could spend our allowance."

Abi smiled. "Sounds like fun. I'll just put my folder back in our room. Should I meet you at the school gate?"

Sasha nodded.

As Abi hurried out of the library, she saw Marsha coming toward her. Marsha glanced at the folder under Abi's arm but said nothing.

When Abi entered her room, Flame sat up and stretched. He made a little sound of greeting.

"Hello, you." Abi gave him a cuddle. "Did you sleep well? I'm just going into town with Sasha. Do you want to come?"

Flame gave an eager meow. Abi opened her bag and he jumped in.

"Comfortable?" she said, putting on her bag. "Let's go."

Sasha was at the gate. She waved as Abi approached.

It was a warm afternoon. Flame stuck his head out of the bag, enjoying the view as Abi and Sasha walked down the road. The town was a cluster of small houses grouped near an old stone bridge that spanned the river.

"There's the store," Abi said, walking across to a large, thatched cottage that stood by itself. As she and Sasha opened the shop door, a bell rang.

Abi felt Flame jump out of her
backpack as he went off looking for
exciting smells to explore.

"Oh, no," Sasha whispered. "Look
who's over there."

Abi saw Keera flipping through some

magazines. Marsha and Tiwa were at the counter buying chips and drinks.

"Just ignore them. Come on," Abi said, walking toward a display of candy. Sasha followed her. She picked up a bag of lemon drops. "My favorites."

Keera looked up. Abi saw her nudge Marsha and then the three of them drifted over.

Abi's heart sank, but she looked straight at Keera.

"Well, if it isn't the tattletale," Keera jeered. She put her hands on her hips. "Marsha saw you doing extra work. You're just trying to get ahead of everybody in class."

"I'm not!" Abi said. "I'm just trying to keep up."

"Oh, yeah, sure!" Tiwa scoffed.

"Leave her alone. She doesn't have to explain herself to you," Sasha spoke up bravely.

"Who asked you?" Marsha turned to Sasha. "I wouldn't buy any candy if I were you. You might get even more spots!"

Keera and Tiwa laughed.

Sasha hung her head. She put a hand up to cover the birthmark on her cheek.

Abi felt her temper rising. She leaped to her friend's defense. "Leave her alone! She doesn't have spots. It's just a birthmark!"

Marsha jutted her head forward. "Listen to the tattletale sticking up for Spotty. Spo-tty! Spo-tty!" she chanted.

She knocked the bag of candy out of Sasha's hands.

"Oh!" Sasha said with dismay as the bag burst. Candy rolled everywhere.

Abi saw a flash of sparks as Flame leaped onto a nearby shelf. He twitched his whiskers and a fountain of silver sparks shot toward Marsha.

Abi felt her backbone start to prickle. "Uh-oh . . . now what?" she said under her breath.

There was a horrible squeaking noise. First one purple blob appeared on Marsha's cheek, then another. Big blotches began popping up all over Marsha's face!

Chapter
FIVE

Keera and Tiwa stared at Marsha in horror.

"What's wrong with your face?" Tiwa said.

"What do you mean?" Marsha went and looked at herself in the glass window. Her face was completely purple and her nose looked all lumpy, like a blackberry. "Oh no! What's happened to me?" she wailed.

"It's probably the Black Death. Stay away from me!" Keera said.

"It might be contagious!" Tiwa backed away.

Marsha burst into tears.

Abi even felt a little sorry for her. She grabbed Sasha's arm and hurried toward the counter. "Quick! Let's pay for our candy and go!"

Marsha clapped her hands to her face. Moaning, she stumbled past the counter and tried to open the door with her elbow.

"Are you all right, dear?" The store owner looked at her with concern.

"Mnnnff," mumbled Marsha, pulling her school sweater over her head.

Keera and Tiwa dashed for the door. Abi saw Keera grab some bags of candy from the counter while the shopkeeper wasn't looking.

Outside the store, Abi told Sasha what she had seen. "Keera stole them! I saw her shove them in her bag!"

"That's awful. Keera gets a lot of allowance. She was bragging about it at lunch. Those three are so mean." Sasha looked toward Keera and Tiwa who were running down the road. Marsha was walking more slowly, trying to keep her face covered. "It's weird what happened to Marsha, isn't it?" She grinned. "But it serves her right!"

Abi nodded and grinned back. "Yes! But I bet it won't last long. It's probably just an allergy or something."

Sasha still looked puzzled. "Some strange things have been happening at school lately, right?"

"Mmm," Abi said, looking away.

Suddenly they both heard some shouting. It was coming from near the river. A group of boys were pointing up at a tree. Two of them were nudging each other and laughing. One of them, the biggest, who looked like he was thirteen, was collecting stones.

"What are they doing?" Abi said.

Sasha shaded her eyes and looked into the tree. "Oh, no! There's a black-and-white kitten up there."

Abi's heart lurched in her chest. It was Flame!

She realized that Flame must have slipped out of the shop and gone exploring. Climbing the tree had been so exciting that he'd forgotten to stay invisible. Now everyone could see him, so he couldn't do any magic to save himself!

Just then Flame slipped. Abi heard him give a yowl of terror as he only just managed to catch onto a branch hanging out over the river. He clung desperately, his back legs dangling in the air.

"He's going to fall!" Abi gasped. Leaping forward, she raced toward the boys.

The tough-looking boy had grabbed a stone. He drew his arm back and took aim.

"No!" Abi screamed.

She rushed up and shoved the tough-looking boy hard in the chest. He was so surprised that he backed off in amazement.

Abi stood beneath the branch, arms outstretched over the river. She was just in time.

Flame gave a howl and fell out of the tree. Abi caught him, hardly noticing as

his sharp claws scratched her hands and arms.

"I've got you, Flame. You're safe," she whispered. She cradled his trembling body.

The tough boy had recovered from his surprise and his face darkened with anger. "Hey, you!" he shouted at Abi.

"Get her, Craig!" one of the other boys called.

Abi realized that Craig was much bigger than her. She glanced at Sasha, who had just reached the tree. "Run!" she yelled.

Sasha didn't need telling twice. She and Abi ran off down the road. Flame nestled against Abi, shivering with fright.

The boys ran after them.

"Look!" Sasha pointed across a field. "That's the back of our school. It must be a shortcut!"

Abi spotted a fence. "Over here!" she urged.

She and Sasha climbed up and jumped into the field. Breathing hard, they bounded across the grass. Abi ran as fast as she could, but holding Flame slowed her down. She looked over her shoulder.

Craig was gaining on her!

Sasha reached the gates. She dragged them open and raced toward the school. "We'll be okay now!" she called over her shoulder to Abi.

Abi had one foot inside the gates. Suddenly she was jerked to a halt.

Craig had grabbed her arm!

Abi struggled to pull free. She couldn't push Craig away or she might drop Flame.

Craig's fingers dug into her arm. "Give me that kitten!" he said through gritted teeth.

"No!" Abi winced, her heart pounding. She curled her arms around Flame and struggled to get away, but Craig was too strong.

Flame gave a tiny meow and a couple of silver sparks shot out of his fur. Abi felt a weak tingle up her spine. Flame was feeling better and trying to do some magic.

She gathered all her strength and gave a final wrench. Taken by surprise, Craig lost his grip. Abi made a frantic dive inside the gates.

Behind her, Craig gave a yell. "Help! I'm stuck!"

Abi turned around. Craig's feet seemed rooted in the ground. He shook his knees, trying to make his legs move. She watched his friends run up and grab his hands. They tried to pull Craig free, but he was stuck fast.

"You big bully!" Abi shouted to Craig as she zoomed down the school path after Sasha. She knew the spell would wear off soon.

Abi didn't look back until she was inside the building. Half a minute later, she collapsed against a wall and tried to catch her breath.

"You were brave," Sasha puffed beside her. "That horrible Craig boy was a lot

bigger than you!"

Abi didn't feel brave. Now that the danger was past, her legs felt weak. The scratches on her hands and arms were stinging like crazy, too.

"When did you let that kitten go?"
asked Sasha.

"What?" Abi realized that Flame
must have made himself invisible. That
meant he was feeling back to his old self.
"Oh, he jumped down back there in the
field," she said quickly. "I bet he lives
somewhere close. He'll find his way back.
I'm just going up to the room. I want to
wash these scratches."

Sasha decided she was hungry and
went off to get some sandwiches. "I'll
bring some up to the room for you."

"Okay. Thanks. And could you get
some milk, please?" Abi began climbing
the stairs.

In her room, Abi sat on her bed with

Flame in her lap. He snuggled up close. "You saved me, Abi. Thank you. But are you hurt?" he meowed with concern.

Abi looked at the deep scratches on her hands. She shrugged. "It doesn't matter."

Flame reached out a paw and touched her very gently. Tiny silver sparks, like Christmas glitter, sprinkled her hands and arms. Abi felt them grow warm. The pain faded. Where the scratches had been, there were now just faint marks.

"Thank you, Flame," she said. "I almost died when I saw you up that tree!"

She bent her head and Flame touched her chin with the tip of his cold black nose. A warm glow settled in Abi's heart. She realized how fond she was of the magic kitten. It made her sad to think that one day he may have to leave.

Chapter
SIX

Abi and Sasha were just finishing classes the following day when they were called to Mrs. York's office.

Keera, Tiwa, and Marsha were already there. Marsha's face had gone back to normal.

Mrs. York explained that Mrs. Brown from the store had noticed that some candy had gone missing. "She's positive it was just after the five of you left her store yesterday afternoon. Do you have anything to say?" she asked.

"I had nothing to do with it," Keera said quickly.

Abi's eyes widened. She looked across at Sasha, but by silent agreement neither of them spoke. Abi didn't want to tell on anyone, even if it was Keera and her horrible friends. Sasha obviously thought the same way.

Tiwa and Marsha were also silent.

Mrs. York looked angry and disappointed. "I'm going to give the person responsible a chance to own up. You have until tomorrow morning. After that, I will take steps to find the truth."

In the hallway outside, Keera smirked at Abi and Sasha. She went off with her friends. They heard them laughing together.

Sasha clenched her fists. "Ooh! They
make me so mad!" she said. "I really
feel like going back and telling the head
teacher that Keera took that candy."

Abi frowned. "Me too, but I'm not going to. I hate what Keera did. But I'm not a snitch."

"But we can't let her get away with it!" Sasha said.

"She won't. My mom says that the truth has a way of getting out," Abi said. "Sorry, Sasha, but I really have to go now. It's basketball practice tonight . . ."

"And you still have that project on ancient Egyptians to work on, right?" Sasha guessed. "I was going to computer club, but I can go later. I'll give you a hand."

"Thanks. You're the best friend anyone could have!" Abi linked arms with Sasha.

By the next morning, no one

had owned up to stealing the candy. Somehow the news had gotten out and rumors were all over the school.

"I heard that Mrs. York is going to do a room search," Sasha said to Abi when they were eating lunch. "Maybe Keera will own up before that."

"I wouldn't hold my breath," Abi said. "But I think she might have a guilty conscience."

"How do you know?" Sasha asked.

"She left basketball practice early to go and see the nurse with a headache," Abi replied.

"Did she?" Sasha looked surprised. "I saw her and Tiwa outside our room just before you got back. She seemed okay then."

Just as Abi was finishing her baked potato and salad, she heard someone call her name. "Mrs. York wants to see you," a girl she had seen around school a few times told her.

Abi rose to her feet. She threw a puzzled glance at Sasha. What could Mrs. York want with her?

"Grounded for a week! But I didn't do anything!" Abi burst out.

She stood in her room, looking with dismay at Mrs. York. The head teacher held up three bags of candy, which she had just found under Abi's bed. "Then how do you explain these?"

"But they're not mine," Abi insisted. "Someone must have put them there."

Keera! *She hid the candy under my bed*, Abi thought. That's why she left basketball practice early!

"Please. You have to believe me. I didn't steal that candy," Abi said.

Mrs. York shook her head. "I'm sorry you still can't seem to tell me the truth. I expected more of you, Abi. I'll have more to say about this later." She left the room.

Stung by the unfairness of it, Abi sank onto a chair. How was she going to prove her innocence?

"Caught red-handed, were you?" said a gloating voice from the doorway. "I wouldn't be surprised if they picked someone else to be captain of the basketball team now."

Abi didn't look up. "Just go away, Keera," she said in a shaky voice.

Over the next week, Abi tried to throw herself into her schoolwork. But it was no use. She couldn't seem to concentrate.

"Keera's telling everyone that you're the thief. We can't let her get away with this!" Sasha fumed at the end of a math class. "I've had enough. I'm going to see Mrs. York right now!"

Abi put her things back into her pencil case. "It's too late for that. Mrs. York will just think you're sticking up for me. She'll never believe me after she found the candy under my bed."

"If only there was some way to make Keera tell the truth," Sasha said.

An idea suddenly sprang into Abi's mind. She sat up straight. "That's it! You're brilliant, Sasha!"

"I am?" Sasha blinked at her.

Abi's idea was taking shape. She grinned. "Remember that first day, how

Keera tried to scare us about the school ghost?"

Sasha nodded. "The Gray Lady."

"Exactly!" Abi said. "I think I might have a way to scare Keera into telling the truth. But I'll need your help."

"Fine. Just tell me what to do," Sasha said.

"Okay. This is the plan . . ."

When Abi had finished, a slow smile spread over Sasha's face. "I think I get the idea!"

That evening, Abi rolled up her bed sheet, tucked it under her arm, and set off with Flame. They made their way along the twists and turns of the old stairways, up to the dusty landing. There were the narrow windows of thick, greenish glass that Abi remembered. In front of her was the ancient wooden door.

As Abi opened it, it seemed to groan in protest. She gave a small shiver. It was creepier up here than she remembered, especially in the fading light.

She wrapped herself in the sheet. "Okay. Do you remember what to do?" she asked Flame.

Flame nodded and gave her a whiskery grin. "I am ready."

Abi heard footsteps on the stairs. "Quick! They're coming!"

She pushed the door so that it almost closed. Slipping the sheet over her head, she melted into the shadows. Little prickles of warmth tickled her spine. Beside her, Flame began to crackle and fizz with silver sparks.

"I'm going back. We're completely lost!" Keera's sulky voice echoed in the stairwell.

"It's just up here, honest. The room's full of awesome sports equipment," Sasha said. "I found it by accident. No one else knows about it."

"Okay, but you'd better be right about this," Keera warned.

"Wait for it," Abi whispered to Flame.

As Sasha pushed the door wide open, it gave a loud creak.

"Now!" Abi hissed.

She felt herself rising in the air. Higher and higher she floated.

"Whoo-oo-oh!" she wailed, flapping her arms. "Keera Moore. I know you stole that candy," she said in what she hoped was a ghostly voice.

"Aargh!" Keera screamed. "Leave me alone. I'm sorry I stole them!"

"You must own up to what you did," Abi said, sounding as spooky as she could.

"All right. Please don't haunt me, Gray Lady!" Keera pleaded.

Abi heard a scuffle and then footsteps running down the stairs. Keera had run away!

"Okay, you can let me down," she whispered to Flame. She drifted down and felt her feet touch the ground. Throwing off the sheet, she gave Flame a quick cuddle. "That was great! Thanks, Flame."

Flame meowed softly. "You are welcome."

Sasha was waiting on the landing when Abi stepped out of the dark room. She grinned broadly. "You were great! I wish you could have seen Keera's face! I thought she was going to faint with fright! Even I was scared. It looked like you really were floating."

"It must have been a trick of the light," Abi improvised. "Bet you a week's allowance that Keera's on her way to see Mrs. York right now!"

Chapter
SEVEN

Abi and Sasha had a break before the next class. They had taken some drinks and chips outside. It was a warm day and they sat on the grass.

"I can't believe Mrs. York let Keera stay on the basketball team," Sasha said. "And she only got grounded for a couple of days! Just because she put on a big act and went and said sorry to Mrs. Brown at the candy store."

"I know. It doesn't seem fair, does it? I hate to admit it, but we'd really miss having Keera on the team. She's a really good player," Abi said. "Anyway, I'm just happy that my name's cleared."

"Me too. How's basketball going?" Sasha asked.

"Really good. Miss Green's a great teacher. She makes you want to do your best," Abi said. "She says the team's starting to play together as a unit. And she thinks we've got a chance of beating the other schools in the tournament."

"That's great," Sasha said. "It's not that far away, is it?"

Abi shook her head. "No. I can't believe we're halfway through the semester. It's gone by so quickly."

Sasha leaned back on her elbows, enjoying the sunshine. She watched

Keera, Marsha, and Tiwa walk past in the distance.

Abi glanced at Flame. He was chasing a butterfly, batting at it with his front paws. It fluttered away and he rolled over and began biting his tail. She chuckled, feeling a surge of affection for him.

"What are you laughing at?" asked Sasha.

"Oh, nothing," Abi replied.

Sometimes, she forgot that no one else could see Flame. But she never forgot how important it was to keep him a secret. Somewhere out there, fierce cats from Flame's own world were searching for him. And if they ever found him, they would kill him.

The next few weeks passed quickly. Abi hardly had time to think. She concentrated on keeping up with her schoolwork and fitting in basketball practice in any spare moments, and then, one morning, she awoke with a sinking feeling.

"We get our results for our schoolwork today," she whispered to

Flame while Sasha was in the shower. "I just know I'm going to get bad grades."

Flame licked her hand with his rough little tongue. "But you have worked hard," he sympathized.

"I know. I've done tons of extra work. But I'm not sure it'll be enough."

Flame looked up at her with big, round eyes. "I can fix this for you," he meowed helpfully.

Abi shook her head. She tickled his ears. "No. That would be cheating. Thanks, anyway, Flame. But I have to face up to this one myself." She flung back the blanket and jumped out of bed. "Come on. Let's go outside for a walk. There's plenty of time before breakfast."

Flame jumped down eagerly.

Sunshine streamed into the room as Abi put on her school clothes and dragged a brush through her hair. Once outside, she and Flame crossed the soccer field and went toward the woods.

Flame ran around the woods, his ears laid flat to his head. He chased wind-blown leaves and sniffed all the exciting smells in the grass.

Abi relaxed as she smiled at his antics. He loved exploring outside.

She had a sudden thought. "Do you have trees and grass where you come from?"

"Yes. And rivers. And mountains. But no people. Just my kind," Flame told her.

A world with only cats, Abi thought, *how strange that must be.* She would love to see it.

Flame seemed to know what she was thinking. "Magic will take me back to my world one day. I do not know when

but I do know it will only be strong
enough for one," he said sadly.

Abi felt disappointed, but she forced
a smile. "Never mind. I don't suppose
there would be much to eat. I bet you
don't have stores!" she joked.

Flame gave her a whiskery grin. "We do not need stores for juicy prey!"

A piece of silvery paper blew toward Abi. She picked it up and crumpled it into a ball and then threw it across the grass. Flame scampered after it. He rolled over and over, hitting at the paper ball with his front and back paws.

Abi laughed fondly. It was so perfect having Flame here. She didn't want anything to ever change.

Chapter
EIGHT

"Abi, come and look. It's our results!"
Sasha called Abi over to the bulletin board
outside the classroom. They had just
finished a math class.

"What does it say?" Abi hardly dared
look.

"You're tenth out of the whole class.
And you got top grades for your ancient
Egypt project," Sasha read.

"Really? That's fantastic!" Abi's spirits
soared. She felt like she could jump to the
moon.

"You deserve it," Sasha said generously.

"Thanks," Abi said. "But I couldn't have done it without your help. Wow! Look at your grades. You're second in the class. I bet your mom and dad will be really proud."

Sasha blushed, but she smiled. "I'm sure they will. I'm really looking forward to seeing them for the holidays."

Abi nodded. "School's great, isn't it? But I miss my mom and dad, too."

"You'll see them in a few days, won't you? At the basketball tournament?" Sasha reminded her.

"Oh, yes. They're coming to watch. It's going to be great. I'm on my way to practice now. There're only a couple left."

Sasha walked part of the way with her.

She stopped by an open classroom with rows of computers. Sasha was helping to design the programs for the tournament.

"See you later," Sasha said. "Have a good practice."

★

In the gym, Miss Green chose squads for a practice match. Abi played in goal attack position and Keera was goal shooter. They worked well together on the court, feeding each other to score points.

"Well played, you two," Miss Green said. "Keep up the good work."

Abi and Keera made their way in silence to the showers afterward. Abi had enjoyed the game. "You're a really good player, Keera," she said a bit reluctantly.

Keera looked surprised. "Thanks," she said. There was a long pause and then she said quietly, "You're not bad yourself."

Abi blinked at her. Keera was being almost human! Maybe she really had learned her lesson and decided to change.

Wait until she told Sasha!

When Abi got back to their room,
Sasha was already there.

"How was computer club?" Abi asked
brightly.

"Oh . . . er, it was okay, thanks." Sasha
had her head down. She reached across to

the bedside table for a tissue and blew her nose.

Abi could tell she had been crying. "What's wrong?"

"I just got a phone call from my mom and dad." Sasha gulped back tears. "They won't be coming home. They have an important business deal to do or something. So I have to stay at school over the holidays."

"Oh, no. What a shame!" Abi sat down next to Sasha and put her arm around her shoulder. "Maybe it won't be so bad. I bet there'll be other girls staying here, too."

Sasha nodded miserably. "I know. But it won't be the same as going home, will it?"

Abi had to agree that it wouldn't.
She would hate to have to stay at school
when semester ended. Poor Sasha.

While she finished eating dinner,
Abi thought about how she could cheer
Sasha up.

The dining room was full of laughter and chatting voices. But Sasha took no notice. She pushed her food around on her plate. It was chocolate pudding, her favorite, but she had eaten only a spoonful.

"Do you want to walk into town?" Abi suggested.

Sasha shook her head. "I don't really feel like it."

Abi tried again. She reached into her backpack. "I've got a great new wildlife magazine. You can read it first, if you like."

Sasha shrugged, but then she took the magazine. "Okay. Thanks."

★

"I'm worried about Sasha," Abi said later to Flame. "I really want to make her feel better, but I don't know what to do."

Flame rubbed his head against her chin, making little comforting noises. "Sasha is sad. Magic cannot help her," he meowed.

"No," Abi agreed, petting him gently. "I don't suppose it can."

She frowned, thinking hard. There had to be something she could do. Suddenly an idea came to her. "I've got it! I know what to do to cheer her up!"

Chapter
NINE

When Abi awoke the next day, she couldn't wait to put her plan into action. She would have to speak to her mom and dad about it first, but today was the day of the tournament and they would be here soon. She couldn't wait.

Abi looked out of the window as the first cars arrived. A banner hung over the parking lot entrance. It read: "Welcome to the Brockinghurst School Tournament."

Abi felt really excited. The previous afternoon, the whole school had worked together on getting ready for the festival. She had helped set out chairs in the gym and put up fliers. Sasha had put programs on all the chairs.

Even Keera, Marsha, and Tiwa did their share.

"Those three seem really different," Sasha commented.

"Yes," Abi agreed. She would have loved to explain how Flame had secretly helped her and Sasha to teach them a lesson!

"Should we go down? I'm helping with welcoming and signing-in," Sasha said.

"I'll come down in a minute," Abi said. When Sasha had left, she turned to Flame. "Are you coming to watch the game?" she asked eagerly.

Flame was on her pillow. He had
curled up into a tight ball. "I will stay
here," he decided.

"Really? Won't you be bored?" Abi
looked at Flame in astonishment. Usually
he loved to be where any action was.
She bent down and pet the top of his

head. "I have to go. I promised to help Miss Green set out the cones and stuff for the warm up."

Flame raised his head. His eyes seemed troubled. "Be well, Abi. Be strong," he meowed softly.

"I will be. I'm fine," Abi said. "Don't worry about me."

She gave him a quick cuddle before leaving the room. He seemed in a strange mood.

Just as Abi reached the gym she spotted two familiar figures. They waved at her. "Abi, darling!"

"Mom! Dad!" she cried, flinging herself at them for a hug. "It's so good to see you. I have to ask you something. It's about Sasha . . ."

"Whoa there! Slow down, Abi," Mr. West said with a grin. "Start again from the beginning."

Abi took a deep breath and explained her idea to her mom and dad. She

crossed her fingers, waiting nervously for their response.

They both smiled.

"Sounds fine to me," said Mrs. West. She glanced at her husband. "What about you?"

"I think it's a wonderful idea!" Mr. West ruffled Abi's hair.

"Yes!" Abi did a little dance of joy. "Awesome. Sorry. Got to go and get changed. See you later!"

Abi put on her gym shoes. She was setting out cones on the courts when she spotted Sasha near the team benches.

"Sasha!" she called, hurrying over. "I've got something to tell you. You're not staying here for the school holidays."

Sasha looked surprised. "I'm not?"

"No. You're coming home to stay with me. I asked Mom and Dad and they think it's a great idea. What do you think?"

A big grin spread over Sasha's face. Her dark eyes shone. "That's great! I'd love to come. Thanks, Abi."

"I can't wait. We're going to have an awesome time!" Abi gave Sasha a hug.

Just then a voice came through the loudspeaker. It was time for the tournament to begin.

Chapter
TEN

As Abi fastened her jersey and looked around at Keera and her other teammates, the excitement built up inside her.

"Round one," the loudspeaker announced.

As captain, Abi led her squad to the players' benches. She sat watching as the other schools' squads played. Then it was time for their game.

"Let's play ball!" Abi gave the players high fives.

"Good luck, Abi!" Sasha called from the crowd.

Abi's squad played well. They won
their first match by thirty points to
twenty.

"We're through to the next round!
Great job, girls," Miss Green praised them.

Their next match was more challenging. The squad scraped through by only thirty-six points to thirty-four.

The following rounds were tough, but to Abi's and everyone's delight they managed to win every game that came their way.

Abi flopped onto the team bench, red-faced and sweaty. She gulped a drink as she watched the play-off for third and fourth places.

Finally the loudspeaker rang out. "And now, the finals for this year's inter-school tournament."

Keera stood up. She looked across at Abi. "We can win this," she said.

Abi grinned. "Let's do it!"

As Abi's squad ran onto the court, the

school cheered and waved. "Come on, Brockinghurst!"

Abi played for all she was worth. She scored four baskets and Keera scored five. It was the last minute of the game. Abi jumped high at a catch, but she landed awkwardly and her foot went over the sideline.

The umpire blew her whistle. "Penalty!"

The other squad took the throw-in. They scored a point. It was now fourteen points each.

Abi felt furious with herself. What a stupid mistake.

"It's okay," Keera said generously.

Abi threw Keera a grateful smile, but they still needed to score again to win

and there were only a few minutes left to
play.

The players regrouped. Abi caught the
ball and passed to Keera.

Keera spun around and aimed, but it was a difficult angle. There was only one chance to score. Would she be able to do it?

Abi had a better shot. "To me, Keera!" she called.

Keera looked around.

Abi held her breath. Would Keera give away her chance at a winning goal?

With only seconds to go before the whistle, Keera passed to her. Abi aimed. She scored!

The umpire blew the whistle. Abi's team had won the tournament!

Cheering broke out in the gym. "Abi! Abi!" Abi's classmates chanted her name.

"Well played, Abi," Keera said.

Abi smiled. "You gave me the chance

at the winning shot," she said. She took hold of Keera's hand and held it up. "We did it together."

"Abi! Keera!" rang out the cheers.

Keera's cheeks went pink. She gave Abi a hug. Abi returned it, her face glowing. "Friends?" she said.

Keera beamed at Abi. "Don't push it!" she joked.

Abi lined up with Keera and the rest of the squads and Mrs. York presented the certificates. Afterward, there was a special snack on the lawn.

Abi showed her certificate to her parents.

"Great job!" Mrs. West said delightedly. "And you're doing so well in class. You seemed to have settled in here really well."

"I wasn't sure I would at first," Abi said. She turned and linked arms with Sasha. "But now I love it here. And I've made some great friends."

Sasha blushed. She grinned from ear to ear.

Suddenly amid all the celebrations, Abi felt uneasy. Something cold prickled up her spine.

She gasped.

Flame! He must be in danger.

She realized now why he had been acting strangely. She knew she had to get to Flame as soon as she could.

"I . . . I have to do something. I'll be right back!" Abi blurted out an excuse to her parents, already racing for a side door.

Somehow she knew just where Flame would be. She wove through the narrow hallways until she came to the staircase. Dashing up the stairs two at a time, she reached the landing. The dusty old door to the storeroom was wide open.

"Flame? Where are you? Are you okay?" Her eyes searched the darkness, looking for the fluffy black-and-white kitten.

"Abi?" came a deep velvety rumble from the shadows.

A large white lion with glowing white fur stepped forward. He smiled, showing long, sharp teeth.

"Prince Flame!" Abi's breath caught in

her throat. She had almost forgotten how startling he was in his true form.

"You're . . . leaving?" she stammered.

Flame nodded. "Cirrus has come to help me."

Now Abi noticed another older-looking lion. He was gray and had a kind, wise face.

"I must go now. Uncle Ebony's spies are very close," Flame growled.

Abi dashed forward. She clung onto Flame and buried her face in his silky white fur. "Take care," she whispered. She forced herself to let him go and backed away.

Flame's fierce emerald eyes crinkled in a smile. "Abi, you are a good friend. Farewell. I will not forget you."

Silver sparks whirled in the air around
the two lions. The sparks spun faster and
faster, like a tornado. Flame raised a paw
in a final wave. His claws glittered like
crystal, and then he and the older lion
were gone.

Abi stared at the empty space, her heart aching.

She would miss Flame so much, but he was safe and that was the most important thing. It had been awesome to share her first semester with the magic kitten. She would never forget all the fun they'd had. It would remain her secret, forever.

Her eyes pricked with tears, but she blinked them away. She had the holidays with Sasha to look forward to. Smiling at the thought, Abi turned and ran down the stairs.

About the Author

Sue Bentley's books for children often include animals, fairies, and wildlife. She lives in Northampton, England, and enjoys reading, going to the movies, relaxing by her garden pond, and watching the birds feeding their babies on the lawn. At school she was always getting yelled at for daydreaming or staring out of the window—but she now realizes that she was storing up ideas for when she became a writer. She has met and owned many cats and dogs, and each one has brought a special kind of magic to her life.